TAKING THE SPINSTER
The Kidnap Club
SAMANTHA HOLT

Copyright © 2020 by Samantha Holt
All rights reserved. This book or any portion thereof may not be reproduced or used in any manner whatsoever without the express written permission of the publisher except for the use of brief quotations in a book review.

Edited by Destini Reece

Proofed by Dom's Proofreading

Cover Art by Holly Perret, The Swoonies Romance Art

AUTHORS NOTE

Thank you for reading the final book of The Kidnap Club series. I hope you've enjoyed reading them as much as I've loved writing them! If you missed *Capturing the Bride* and *Stealing the Heiress, Taking the Heiress* can still be read as a standalone. You can read about Nash and Grace's story in Book 1 and Russell and Rosamunde's in Book 2. If you enjoy this series, you might also like my *Rogues of Redmere* stories.

Chapter One

GUY GLANCED OVER HIS shoulder and caught a glimpse of the reporter barreling down the London road with all the subtlety of an express coach. She darted behind a wall and his lips twitched with a grin. If she were not such a pain in the rear, he'd find her amusing, but he couldn't afford to have her witnessing the clandestine meeting he was due at, or worse still, linking him to The Kidnap Club.

However, this was tantamount of persecution and it was becoming tiresome.

He picked up the pace, taking long strides down the pavement, keeping his attention fixed ahead. The sun lingered behind the buildings, dipping their squared-off tops in amber frosting. Before long, the streets of the city would be swallowed by darkness, but he had a suspicion even that wouldn't rid himself of her.

He damn well needed to, though. He couldn't very well have a clandestine meeting with a duchess in the park if this nosy London Chronicle reporter continued to follow him.

Guy allowed himself a smirk. Reporter gave her too much credit. Miss Haversham, he had discovered, was the lady behind the gossip column for the Chronicle.

He could count on one hand the amount of times he'd been featured in that very column but even once or twice was enough, especially when the gossip had been about him and Lady A.

Amelia.

Another woman who had done a fine job of being a pain in the rear.

No, he supposed it was more like a pain in the heart. He blew out a breath. The bloody woman still had some sort of hold over him. Whenever he recalled her name, it twisted in his heart, digging the knife of frustration deeper. He'd been so close…had thought just maybe, this was it—he'd finally found a woman who wanted him. All of him.

But, alas, it was not to be.

The pain had eased perhaps over the past few years but it still damn well hurt, and he didn't need a woman like Miss Haversham lapping up all the details of his failed engagement, so eager to expose the heartbreak of the Earl of Henleigh to all of England.

Whatever she wanted with him, he did not want to know. As far as he was concerned, gossip columns were the lowest form of journalism and he would give her no tinder for the godawful fire that was her job.

He stilled once more and feigned glancing up at one of the three-story buildings that blocked out the waning sun—a tall, dark silhouette with windows only lit on the second floor. A shadow moved about in one window, and he spied a gentleman clasping a glass and moving toward the fireplace. Golden light flickered and danced. Guy pulled his coat closer at the neck and gave a shiver.

A warm fire and drop of brandy while seated in his favorite armchair would be wholly welcome at present. Far more appealing than scurrying through the streets of London like a damp rat to a secret meeting. It would have been nice to at least have his carriage, but the crest emblazoned on the side wouldn't help with the whole clandestine nature of it.

Well, he would have that brandy as soon as this was over, he vowed. And as soon as he'd rid himself of Miss Haversham. She currently peeked out from the side of an alleyway.

He exhaled and pinched the bridge of his nose. The woman would not cease. He knew that already. She'd been demanding audiences with him for several months—all of which he'd declined. He had little idea what she wanted with him but given his association and leadership of The Kidnap Club, the less she poked around in his life, the better. Too many women relied on his life remaining a mystery for him to even consider having a conversation with her.

The chances were, of course, she wanted comment on something silly. Like the fact Amelia had married recently.

Why Miss Haversham found amusement in poking about his wounds, he could not say. He didn't know her nor did he want to. After the Amelia debacle, he had resigned himself to the fact that he and women did not mix, nor would they ever. His duties as an earl be damned, he would stay a bachelor forever and ensure his half-brother was legitimized.

Russell might have a thing or two to say about that but there was not much else that could be done. The man would inherit the title and no doubt he and Rosie would have children before long and the line of succession would be safe.

Guy took a few more steps. The streets were quiet, a few pedestrians moving at pace before night swallowed London. A carriage rolled by and a cart soon followed. He darted between the two vehicles, pausing briefly so that he was hidden behind. Then he looped swiftly around.

Miss Haversham moved out of her hiding place and paused, glancing around with her hands to her hips. "Where on earth—" she muttered to herself.

"Looking for me?" Guy came up behind her.

She whirled, her eyes wide, her pale hair warmed a little by the streetlight. "Bugger."

He'd be amused by her bad language if he didn't loathe reporters like her so much. He kept his expression firm, allowing his jaw to harden. He'd intimidated many a man with such an expression.

She lifted her pointed chin, fixed him with her pale blue gaze, and folded her arms.

"Actually, yes, I am."

IF THE EARL WISHED her to be scared, he'd have to try harder. She hadn't survived a year in what was still a man's job only to be cowed by intense eyes, a hard jawline, and furrowed brows.

Her heart did pick up a little, though.

Traitor.

No doubt many a man and woman, perhaps even animal, had cowed at such a look. But not her. He might have about the strongest jaw Freya had ever seen, finished off with a dip in the middle of his chin, or the darkest, thickest brows, complete with permanent furrows between them that made her feel as though she were mightily disapproved of. He might be tall too, with wide shoulders. And of course, all his clothes fit him perfectly, made of the finest fabrics.

But none of that mattered. Not his acceptable looks—because they were merely that—not his coat that would likely cost her a lifetime of earnings, not his dark scowl, not his rather thick lips.

She scowled to herself. Thick lips? Who cared if he had thick lips? Why was that even worthy of note? She shook her head and peered up at him from beneath the brim of her hat.

He glared down at her, the shadows of his own hat making him appear more dark and intimidating than ever.

It wouldn't deter her, though.

She had a story to chase down and she'd be damned if she would let him scare her away from it. This could be her chance to move away from those wretched, insipid gossip columns that she so loathed. Gosh, she could just imagine it. Writing a story about the missing noblewomen and finally getting the respect she craved for her writing. Finally being something in the man's world that was newspapers.

Oh yes, and finally earning enough money to actually keep her parents comfortable in their old age.

So, there it was. A dark look from a titled gentleman was not going to veer her off this path, no matter how much he made her heart race.

"You really should cease following me about, Miss Haversham. It is hardly appropriate behavior."

She resisted the desire to roll her eyes. Appropriate behavior was for ladies of genteel breeding and not working women like her. For as long as she could remember, she had roamed the streets of London, finding vaguely respectable work where she could until she had finally persuaded the editor of the Chronicle to take her on. She had learned to look after herself and she hardly had the time for *appropriate behavior.*

"Lord Huntingdon, all I need is a moment of your time."

He shook his head. "I do not have a moment."

"You've refused all of my audiences."

"Well, yes. When one is an earl, one does tend to be quite busy."

"I just have a few questions—"

He pivoted away. "You should return home, Miss Haversham. It's growing dark."

She moved hastily in front of him, blocking his path. It was a little laughable to think that she, with her average stature and her average looks, average hair, average, well, everything apart from her mind, could hold the rich, entitled, slightly more than acceptable-looking man at bay, but she had never given up easily on anything and she would not start now. Goodness, it had taken months of thrusting her work at her editor and standing outside his office for him to finally look at her writing.

"Miss Haversham, is stalking my footsteps every day really the right way about this?"

She pursed her lips at his condescending tone. "You have refused all of my requests for an audience, my lord, and I really only have a few questions—"

"I have nothing to say about Miss Jenkins." He frowned and rubbed his forehead. "I mean, Mrs. King."

Freya hesitated. "Mrs. King?" She let her lips round. He meant the woman with whom he was to be married. She recalled writing about the broken engagement a few years ago. "Oh no, I do not care about your failed engagement."

Lord Huntingdon winced slightly, the quickest flash of pain.

She cursed inwardly. Most marriages between the upper classes were arranged so she had assumed it had not bothered him when Miss Jenkins ended their agreement but perhaps he had really cared for her. Stranger things had happened after all.

It was rather hard to imagine this stony-faced, glowering man with all his privilege and wealth being able to love anyone but himself, however.

"That is to say, I have questions about another matter."

"Whatever it is, I have no comment on it. I do not care if Lady W is having an affair with a Sir S or if the patrons of Almacks are threatening to bar a certain devious rake from the hallowed dance floor." He locked his gaze to hers. "I, Miss Haversham, have no inclination for gossip."

She didn't normally care if people derided her work. It was merely a means to an end after all. But for some reason it stung, like she'd rolled into a cluster of nettles and now her skin was heated and painful. It shouldn't. Why should she care for the opinion of a man who had never worked a day in his life?

Lifting her shoulders, Freya maintained eye contact with him. "I am not looking for gossip. I am looking for facts. On a particularly important matter."

"Oh yes," he drawled.

"The disappearance of Lady Steele."

Something flickered in his gaze. It might have been a trick of the light streaming from the nearby building, but she didn't think so. Her instincts were rarely wrong, especially when she came across a story, and right now, her instincts were aflame.

He knew something.

"You were one of the last people to be seen with her after all," Freya probed. "Right before she vanished," she added. "That was over four years ago now."

He shrugged. "She was a member of the *ton*. We titled folk do tend to spend some time together, Miss Haversham, as you may have noticed."

"So she did not say anything to you? Did not infer that she was in trouble of any kind? Because you must admit, it is odd. There has been rather a rash of disappearances and kidnappings of wealthy women of late. In fact, there has been at least four that I have—"

He held up a hand. "Miss Haversham, it seems you have quite the fevered imagination. As much as I would like to say that I keep company with many of the beautiful women of the *ton*, I do not. I am a busy man with little time for socializing and frivolities. I'm sorry if that does not feed your column but there you have it." He waved a hand behind her, and she scowled and turned. A carriage rolled up and he jumped in, swiftly tapping the roof.

"Good evening, Miss Haversham," he said as he slammed shut the door of the hack and leaned out of the window. "With haste," he barked at the driver before she could quite fathom what had occurred.

The carriage moved off, leaving her no time to react or grab the door. She dropped her hand and watched the vehicle vanish around the corner. What would she have done had she managed to snatch the door? Hang off the vehicle like a madwoman?

Perhaps.

Well, he might have escaped her tonight, but this would not be the last he saw of her. There was a story behind the quite handsome earl's eyes, and nothing would dissuade her from finding out what it was.

Chapter Two

GUY DITCHED THE CARRIAGE some way from his meeting spot after bellowing the direction to the driver as they moved rapidly through the quiet streets. He peered around the dark roads. Windows glowed and streetlamps were being lit, slowly eating away at the shadows that dominated. The scent of smoke imbued the air as houses ignited their fires to keep away the Autumn chill. A light breeze whipped past him, ruffling his cravat. He tugged his coat tighter around his neck and took one more look around.

A few people moved briskly along the pavement and several carriages rolled by. He eyed each closely. There was no chance Miss Haversham had caught up with him, but he wouldn't put it past the damned woman to sprout wings and fly over the rooftops just to pester him with more questions.

Questions he really could not, would not answer. Questions that were almost worse than *why exactly did Miss Amelia Jenkins end your engagement a mere week before the wedding?*

He could answer that one but well, *she ran screaming from the bedroom* really wasn't an answer he wanted bandied about.

As for the missing women, if he so much as uttered a word to a snooping reporter, all of them could end up in danger.

Somehow, he suspected Miss Haversham would not let the matter drop so he was going to have to conjure a way of putting her off the story.

Damn. He ran a hand over his face and marched toward the park, satisfied no stubborn-chinned woman was following him. How had she even connected the women to him? He had been careful. Ridiculously so. Word of The Kidnap Club was a closely guarded secret and anyone who knew about it had either been kidnapped, sought their help, or was one of their own. Being seen with one of the missing women was hardly a crime, and if he recalled correctly, he had run into Lady Steele accidentally, just prior to her kidnapping, and she had wished to be just as cautious as he.

He stepped through the wrought iron gates of Green Park and made his way to the fountain. In warmer weather, the park would be thronged with pedestrians but at night the dark paths were more often home to footpads and drunkards. Precisely why he had brought his pistol. He could handle himself in most situations, but it never paid to be careless.

When he emerged out of the other side of the park by Piccadilly, a carriage moved forward from the shadows of a side road. The door opened and he stepped into the darkened confines. Shadows masked the woman's face but there was no mistaking the regal bearing of Lady Clearbury, Duchess of Newhampton.

"Your Grace," he greeted, settling opposite her.

The vehicle jerked forward, and he gripped the edge of the open window with a gloved hand.

"Thank you for meeting with me, Henleigh."

He waited, the silence punctuated by the rolling of wheels and the clack of hooves. In his experience, women who came to him struggled to find the words to describe their situations. It was best to leave them unprompted until they found their courage. To seek out his services took enough mettle as it was without a man demanding answers, and he had learned over the past few years to treat these women with a tender hand.

Not that he had ever treated women with a rough hand. Nor would he. He'd seen what those beasts of men could do to women, and if he could string them all up, he would, but, alas, there was no recourse for a man who laid hands on his wife.

Lady Clearbury cleared her throat and twisted her hands together. He'd assumed her marriage a pleasant one. She and the duke appeared close and had been married at least two decades. But appearances could be deceiving. He knew that all too well.

So many thought him to be the classic bachelor. A mistress tucked away somewhere perhaps but most certainly entirely attached to remaining single and making love to all the ladies of the *ton* behind their husbands' backs. The mistaken impression served him well, but it couldn't be farther from the truth.

"I need your assistance," she said, her voice a little hoarse.

"I'm not sure what I can do to aid you," he replied cautiously.

"I think you do." She fixed him with a firm gaze, the passing streetlight highlighting her stern features. "I know you have helped women."

He didn't respond.

"I want you to help my sister."

"Your sister?"

She nodded. "Lady Louisa Pembroke. She is close to your age. No doubt you went to her coming out ball."

"Ah yes." He frowned. "I regret, I have not seen her in years."

"For a good reason." Lady Clearbury tightened her lips. "Her husband controls her every move. She is rarely allowed to go anywhere."

"I see."

"I have not been able to see her for two years." Her voice cracked, and she leaned forward. "The fact is, Baron Pembroke—her husband—is a brute who beats her on a whim. My sister is obedient and was keen to prove herself a fine wife. There is no chance she deserves any kind of cruelty."

"I am of the school of thought that it is never acceptable to raise a hand to a woman, regardless of their behavior," he said firmly.

"Well, you are a rarity, I am afraid."

"How do you know he is treating her this way if you have not seen her?" Guy despised asking these questions, but he had to be certain of the woman's situation before he put himself and the rest of The Kidnap Club at risk.

"She managed to get a letter to me about a month ago. The beatings are getting worse. She said she feared she might die at his hands." She reached into her reticule and tugged out a scrap of paper. She handed over the letter with a shaky hand.

He took it and turned it into the light from the streets. He couldn't read it all, but he saw enough to recognize the severity of the situation.

"I need you to get to my sister, Louisa. Somehow. Any longer trapped in that marriage and I believe her fears will come true." The duchess reached over and grabbed his hand in a fervent grip. "Please say you will do this for me."

Guy didn't need to think twice. He might not have much of an affiliation with women these days and was intent on keeping it that way after the Amelia fiasco, but he'd seen first-hand what these sorts of men did to their wives. He couldn't leave Louisa Windham to her fate, and this was precisely why The Kidnap Club had been formed.

"I'll help you," he vowed.

TUGGING THE PINS FROM her hair, Freya opted to leave her thick coat on as she clustered the pins in her hand and slipped them in her pocket. She ran her fingers through her hair and rubbed her scalp with a sigh of relief. Silly her for trying to look professional. Lord Huntingdon might have treated her more cordially had she looked sweet and lovely, like one of the ladies of the *ton*.

She wrinkled her nose and paused to light the lone candle in the hallway. There was no chance of her looking like any of them, not without money and breeding. Everything about her was pale. Fair hair that looked almost white in some lights and eyes that were only passably blue. Whilst the women of the ton favored a fair complexion, hers tended to look more sickly than delicate.

Alas, she was not without vanity, even though she really ought to be. Looking pleasing meant little for a woman like her. The only way she would get anything in life was with hard work.

That did not stop her wondering how it would feel to have a man like the earl admire her, though?

Freya shook her head at herself and tiptoed down the hallway, pausing at the doorway of the drawing room. The fire offered a weak glow that barely permeated the room let alone the rest of the house. She'd sleep in her threadbare coat tonight seeing as her father hadn't kept the fire going.

She eased past the armchair where she had left her father this morning. A noise rather like the growl of an annoyed dog emanated from his open mouth. She glanced at the dog by his feet. "How come Papa sounds more like a dog than you do?" she whispered.

Brig's ears perked up and he eased slowly to his feet. The bulldog sat at only calf height and moved slowly toward her. She dropped to a crouch, offering out a hand for the half-blind animal as he moved sluggishly toward the scent of her. He gave her a little sniff then butted against her hand. Freya smiled, dropping fully to the floor and allowing the white dog to crawl upon her lap for a good, thorough fuss.

"I really should get this fire going," she told Brig. "We'll all freeze tonight otherwise."

"I only fell asleep for a little while," her father grumbled. "It's not even that cold."

She glanced up to see him straighten in his chair and pull the blanket over him. "Oh is it not? Then I suppose you do not need that blanket."

"I like it," he protested. "It's comfortable."

She rose and placed the dog down on the rug near the waning fire. Her father peered at her through droopy eyelids, his bushy brows nearly covering his vision. Creases and a large, ruddy nose dominated his face while his white hair remained thick.

Sometimes she wished her parents were younger—that she had been born sooner—but no parent could love her as much as they did. *Their little miracle baby.* After twenty years of trying to have a child, she had apparently been a welcome shock to them.

Leaving a fleeting kiss on her father's cheek, she strode over to the fireplace and loaded it with dry twigs then blew on it. Flames sparked to life and she tentatively added a little wood.

"What's the time?" Papa asked, glancing at the clock on the mantel.

"Time for bed."

She smothered a yawn with the back of her hand. Between researching her story and staying up late to finish the gossip column and caring for her parents, she had scarcely had four hours' sleep last night. Add that to goodness how many late evenings of assisting Lucy and she reckoned she hadn't enjoyed a full night's sleep in at least a month.

"How's the story going?" Her father inched up from the chair and winced when a bone cracked. "Good God, never age, Freya. It's extremely tiresome."

"I'll do my best," she said brightly.

He stopped in front of her and cupped her cheek, turning her toward the lamplight. "You look tired, my girl. You need some rest. Trust me, I know more about hard work than anyone, and you will regret it when your bones are as tired as mine." He pressed his lips together. "Though, Lord knows, I would give anything to be able to go back to work so you could enjoy your life a little more."

"I do enjoy my life," she insisted, clasping his hand and removing it from her face. "I love writing and I just know I have a good story here."

"I know you don't like writing those columns."

"They are a start, Papa. I would wager you did not enjoy being a clerk either but look where it got you. You became a solicitor with an excellent reputation."

"If my eyes weren't as bad as Brig's, I'd still be a solicitor," he grumbled.

"You would miss your daytime naps too much," she teased.

"Well, I'm sure I could fit them in around my work," he said with a grin. He glanced at the ceiling. "Have you checked on your mother yet? Lucy came and helped me with supper for her and she was in quite the talkative mood. Your mother that is, though that Lucy could talk the ears off the biggest gossips in Town."

Freya chuckled. She had known Lucy for many years—since Lucy's father had brought her over from the Caribbean as a girl—and they helped each other out where they could. Lucy assisted with her parents while Freya worked, and she aided Lucy with her thriving business as a seamstress to some quite important people. Her friend's reputation had grown of late and she suspected it wouldn't be long before she'd be moving out of Prince's Street. She didn't resent her success one jot but, gosh, she was going to miss being so close by her.

"I'll go and check on Mama in a moment. She's probably sleeping by now."

"I heard her coughing for most of the day."

Freya kept her expression neutral. The last thing her father needed was to be worrying about Mama's health. Unfortunately, after a bout of illness, she had yet to fully recover. "I'm sure some soup or tea will help. I'll go prepare some."

Her father put his hands to her shoulders. "You will go to bed," he ordered. "I'm quite capable of warming some soup."

"But—"

"Go," he commanded, twisting her toward the door by her shoulders. "Knowing you, you shall be rising early in pursuit of this story tomorrow, and I would far rather you chase down villains with a full night's rest."

"Yes, Papa," she intoned, knowing he wasn't wrong. The only question was, was Lord Huntingdon really a villain?

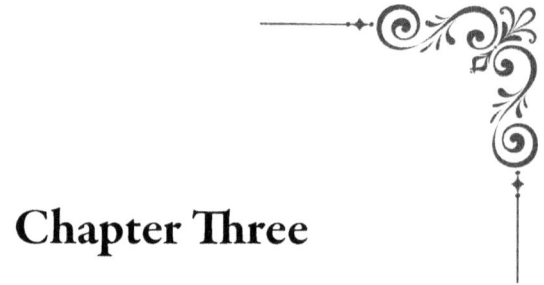

Chapter Three

RUSSELL LIFTED HIS lithe shoulders. "Well, Rosie could try to make contact with Lady Pembroke," he suggested.

Guy eyed his half-brother who stood by the window, keeping watch. The man was no fool and had about the smartest mind of the three members of The Kidnap Club but they were struggling to fathom how to reach the baron's wife. At this point, no one could even say if the woman still lived, such was the rarity of her being seen out in society.

He frowned. Make that five members. Both Russell and Nash had married within the past year and both of their wives assisted with the kidnaps.

"I think it best I try," Guy said. "It sounds as though Lady Pembroke's husband is a brute, and I wouldn't want to put her in danger."

"The damned madwoman practically craves danger," Russell said, easing up from his chair in the dilapidated cottage. "But I trust your judgement, Guy."

While Grace, Nash's wife, helped with looking after the ladies and staying out of danger, Rosamunde took part in the kidnappings. The bold woman did rather a fine job of it too. They had saved another two women from dire situations since

Nash gave him a look. "You are the lost half-brother of the Earl of Henleigh. Of course she will wish to write about you."

"Not if I can help it," Guy muttered. "Though the damned woman has a mind of her own."

"What woman doesn't?" said Nash with a shrug. "I've learned just to go along with it. It's much easier that way."

Russell nodded, a slight knowing smile upon his lips, and unfolded his arms then pushed away from the windowsill. "I concur."

"Well, I won't be going along with Miss Haversham," Guy declared. "It could put all we've worked for at risk, and worse, endanger the women we've aided."

"I'm sure you can manage one little woman," Nash said. "After all, you're the damned Earl of Henleigh."

"I can handle her," Guy murmured. Of course he could. Most definitely. One little pale woman wasn't going to get the better of him. No, sir. "Just keep clear if she does approach you."

"Understood." Russell came to join him at the door. "So I'll see if I can find out anything more about Lady Pembroke and her routine."

"From a distance," Guy reminded him.

"Naturally."

"And I shall go back to my lovely wife in the country and wait for word from you both." Nash paused to glance between them. "You know, I really don't know how Grace and I didn't see the similarities between you two. Especially Grace. She's the smartest woman I know."

Russell made a noise. "We look nothing alike."

"Not obviously no, but there's definitely something there. Around the eyes I think." He gestured with a finger at Russell's face and Russell batted his finger away. "Not to mention you both have the same hair color."

"Nash, one day I'm going to send you back to the country to your dilapidated estate and leave you there," Guy grumbled.

"You wouldn't dare. You need my charm and good looks. Neither of you have any, that's to be certain. You both scare the women we help half to death. Besides, the estate isn't so dilapidated now. It's coming along quite nicely."

"I'll look for my dinner invitation," Guy drawled.

"Well, it's not quite ready for dinner parties," Nash admitted. "But we've made damned good progress."

"Who do you have doing your painting?" Russell asked. "It's just that..."

Guy left before the men could continue their conversation and mounted his horse. He could do without conversations of matrimonial happiness and painting the houses they shared with their wives. Though he certainly didn't resent either of them their happiness, it was a sore reminder that he'd never have the same. No woman would go near him if Amelia's reaction to him was anything to go by.

THIS STORY HAD TO BE worth it. It just had to.

Worth the water slowly seeping into the hole in her left boot and the raindrops dripping down the back of her coat from the brim of her hat. Worth at least two hours standing in the rain now. But the newspaper boy said he'd seen the earl's carriage leave earlier in the day and Freya had no intention of letting him escape her again.

Huddled under a tree, she eyed every passing carriage in anticipation of spotting the earl's crest. She glanced down at her muddied hems. Wearing her smartest muslin dress had been a mistake. The pale fabric soaked up half the puddles, leaving her with skirts that went from white to light brown to a nice dark mud color. She grimaced. How was she ever going to get the earl to take her seriously when she looked as though she had traipsed across a muddy field?

Well, it didn't matter now. She caught sight of the crest that she didn't think she would ever forget. She'd studied this man intimately and there was something odd about him. He behaved like a bachelor yet there were no scores of heartbroken women behind him. Even the circumstances behind his broken engagement were odd. Miss Amelia Jenkins had, as far as she could tell, been thrilled with the match and quite in love with the man. So why she should have a change of heart at the last minute, Freya could not fathom.

She had to conclude a mildly attractive man like the earl had lovers somewhere. A gentleman like him did not just live life without female company. Goodness knows, she had written about enough affairs and titillations to last a lifetime. But where these lovers were, she did not know. Not even a hint of something more scandalous and illegal could be found.

There was a story here, though, of that she was certain. He knew something about these missing women, and she wouldn't let him brush her off again.

Stepping straight into the street, she held up her hands. The carriage bore down upon her, raindrops sliding off the sleek black exterior. The ground vibrated underfoot as the two horses neared. She had anticipated the driver stopping much sooner but the vehicle barreled on. Breath held, she winced, bracing herself for a collision.

What a stupid, foolish hill this would be to die on.

Her heart dropped practically down to her toes when the carriage came to an abrupt halt of whinnying horses and a cursing driver.

"What the bloody hell do you think you're playing at?" he demanded.

She waved a hand at him and skirted around the carriage, tugged open the door and hauled herself up into it. She plopped down onto the cushioned seat opposite the earl.

He eased his newspaper down, a dark brow lifting. She supposed some women might find the look a little titillating. How he fixed her with his grey-blue eyes made her chest a little tight. But, no, that was more likely from nearly being trampled to death. She pressed a hand to her chest and offered a quick smile.

"My lord," she said breathlessly.

He folded the paper and set it on the seat then tapped the roof. "Continue on."

She put her palm to the plush seat as the vehicle rocked into motion once more. "I rather thought you might sling me out."

"Tempting." He cast his gaze over her. "You rather look like you have already had enough splashes in puddles though."

Her cheeks burned. She shouldn't care what he thought of her appearance. After all, how could she compete with silks and feathers and diamonds? However, a tiny, teeny weeny part of her wished that maybe she could experience such things. Only once. She wasn't greedy after all. How would it feel to be beautiful and glamorous and admired by someone like the earl, she wondered.

With a shake of her head, she focused her attention on the earl. "I've been waiting for some time for you."

"I knew I should have continued on horseback," he muttered.

"Pardon?"

"Nothing." He laced his gloved hands over a knee. "What do you want, Miss Haversham? I'm a—"

"Busy man." She held up a hand. "I know."

"Well get to it."

"An audience with you, that's all I ask."

His mouth tightened. "You have one now."

"A proper one. One where I am not soaked to the bone and where I can ask you my questions."

His gaze flickered over her and the permanent furrow between his brows deepened. He plucked a blanket up from beside him and before she had quite fathomed what had occurred, he draped the beautifully soft wool about her shoulders.

He moved back swiftly, giving her the briefest moment to inhale the subtle scent of him. He smelled of sandalwood and a little mint. For some odd reason, that scent made her stomach do a little twirl.

Or perhaps it had been his proximity.

She shoved away the thought. It couldn't have been any of that. More likely, the taste of a story so close by had her all on edge.

"I..." She pressed her lips together. "Um, that is..."

"I don't know anything about those women. I saw Lady Steele just before her disappearance and she seemed entirely normal with no hint as to why she might vanish. And I cannot tell you anything more I'm afraid." He leaned back. "Does that satisfy?"

"Satisfy?" she repeated, her voice slightly strangled.

Something lingered behind his eyes that told her he knew precisely how to satisfy. Which made it all the more puzzling why she could not find a history of lovers trailing behind him. She pushed the blanket off her shoulders as warmth flowed suddenly through her. He watched the movement with a bemused look. Damn the man, he had to know what he was doing to her.

And damn her for falling for it. She was not some innocent debutante with flowers in her hair. She was eight and twenty for goodness sakes. A spinster of little means. She had no time for the charms of a privileged man.

"Lord Huntingdon, I would request once more for an audience with you so I can ask you my questions properly." And she would not have to be in such close confines with the almost handsome man.

The earl rubbed a hand across his jaw, drawing her attention to the stubble that lingered there, implying it either grew swiftly or he had left in a rush this morning without shaving.

"Miss Haversham?"

Freya lifted her gaze to his. "Yes?"

"I asked if Tuesday would suffice. At two o'clock?"

"Oh. Yes. Of course." She fought a silly grin from spreading across her face. "That would be wonderful." She paused. "I mean, that would be acceptable."

"Excellent." He tapped on the roof and opened the door when the carriage drew to a halt. "Good day, Miss Haversham." He jerked his head toward the open door.

She came to her feet swiftly, dragging the blanket with her. "Oh." She tugged it off her shoulder and tried to hand it back to him, but he shook his head.

"Keep it."

"But—"

"Keep it, Miss Haversham."

Scowling, she gripped the blanket in one hand, ducked out of the carriage and jumped down into a puddle that soaked instantly through her boot. She turned to thank him, but the carriage rolled off swiftly.

With a sigh, she glanced furtively around the quiet street and she gave the wool a little sniff. Sandalwood. Just like him.

Chapter Four

"YOU'RE GOING TO BE late, my lord."

Guy glared at the butler's head. Glaring directly at him was hard as Brown stood a good two feet shorter than he. His small stature didn't diminish his capabilities, however.

Oh no, the butler did a fine job of ordering him about almost as well as Mrs. Bellamy, his housekeeper. Between them, Guy had a good suspicion he knew exactly what it was like to have overbearing parents. Given his own mother preferred to reside in sunnier climates and his father had been dead many years, he couldn't decide if that was a good thing or not.

Brown lifted his head and met his stare, his blue eyes still bright for a man of older years though surrounded by lined eyes and white, barely there eyebrows. Little tufts of white clung stubbornly to his forehead in a pattern not unlike that of an exotic animal. His hair mimicked his brows but offered up darker patches that Guy could swear made the shape of an animal if one stared at it long enough.

"My lord?" Brown offered out a scarf.

Guy blinked. "Oh yes."

"You seem incredibly distracted at present, my lord."

"Nonsense," Guy scoffed.

Brown leaned in, giving him a full view of the black and white patchwork of his scalp. "Anything to do with that woman who keeps requesting an audience? Mr. Newport said she stepped in front of your carriage the other day. Nearly made him keel over in shock."

Guy increased his glare. "It certainly isn't, and I would warn you against gossiping with Mr. Newport, Brown."

"Well, someone has to tell me what you are doing with your life. Goodness knows, you never tell me anything."

"I don't have to," Guy protested.

"If it were not for me, you wouldn't know if you were coming or going."

"I am most definitely going. Right now." He snatched the scarf and flung it around his neck, cinching it so tight he swore he'd burned himself on the fabric.

He strode out of the townhouse, down the long path between fading flowers and the evergreen bushes that protected the house from the view of the busy London street. What the devil was Brown on about? He hadn't been distracted. Not one jot.

Wind blew a splatter of rain sideways at him. He grimaced and recalled Miss Haversham's shaking shoulders after standing for so long in similar weather. No doubt she was out in the rain, doing whatever it was female reporters did. Most likely pestering some other poor soul about a story. The bloody woman needed to move onto a different story or go back to her inane gossip. Surely one didn't need to stand in the pouring rain to write about the ins and outs of fashionable society?

He pressed his lips together. The woman needed a thicker coat too. Part of him had wanted to march her to the nearest seamstress and order a thick, lined coat for her so he wouldn't ever have to see her shivering away like that again.

Damn it. He didn't even wish to see her again. After their meeting—

He came to a stop at the end of the path and let his expression sour. Had he conjured her? "Miss Haversham."

Standing on the other side of the gate, a black umbrella held unsteadily in one hand, she fought with the latch. "My lord," she said, frustration inching into her voice when she pressed her legs into the gate, and it refused to budge. A flurry of wind blasted across the garden, rustling her skirts and nearly lifting her simple brown bonnet from her head. She huffed and tried again.

With a shake of his head, Guy closed the distance between them and flipped open the latch, drew the gate open, stepped aside and gestured for her to enter with a flourish.

She gave him a tight smile. "Thank you. I—" Wind caught her umbrella, turning it inside out and nearly tearing it from her arm. "Oh!"

"Turn it into the wind," he ordered over the gust that curled around them. "Into the wind, damn it," he repeated when she twisted the wrong way and nearly took his nose off.

"Oh." She twisted again but the umbrella gave a wild flap back and forth before popping back the wrong way around.

Sighing, he went to snatch it from her but as he grabbed it, she swiveled, connecting one of the spokes with his face. He winced, feeling it scrape across his cheek. She froze and the umbrella gave one last fluttering fight before popping the right way around. Miss Haversham quickly closed it.

"Oh dear." She scrabbled in her reticule then drew out a handkerchief and went to dab his cheek with it.

He retreated, away from her outstretched hand.

"You're bleeding!"

He pressed fingers to his cheek, and they came away red. Blast. He couldn't go to the solicitors practically dripping blood. Holding a hand to his cheek, he glowered at her. "What are you doing here anyway?"

"Our meeting." Her pale eyebrows lifted. "You recall? Tuesday at two o'clock."

"Ah."

How could he have forgotten? Usually—with some help from Brown of course—he counted himself as extremely organized and he couldn't fathom how he had forgotten he'd agreed to speak with the fair-haired wild woman that was Miss Haversham.

Admittedly, he had spent some time thinking of her. Time that he really should not have been wasting dwelling on a pesky writer. It was just his mind hadn't gone to the important things. It had been wasted on pondering what sort of figure lay underneath that threadbare coat. Or how spikey her lashes had been when damp, drawing attention to her pale eyes and making her look a little ethereal. Her skin was so pale it was almost translucent, leaving little dark smudges under her eyes. He couldn't decide if that was from cold, lack of sleep or was just naturally her.

"I am rather busy," he started.

Miss Haversham took another step forward and practically slapped the handkerchief to his face, pinning it there. "Well now you need nursing so whatever your plans were, you should cancel them." She paused and a smug smile crossed her lips. "And then you can answer my questions."

Guy groaned inwardly.

A MAN SMALLER THAN Freya peered at them as she hustled Lord Huntingdon in through the front door, still holding the handkerchief to his cheek.

"Take the damned umbrella from her, Brown," the earl ordered. "She's a menace with it."

One uneven brow lifted, and the butler took the offending object from her. "Anything else, my lord?"

"No, I'll handle this."

The way he said *this,* she knew he meant her. The very idea of him handling her set a tiny, warming fire in her belly. She doused it quickly and reminded herself precisely why she was here. Fancy wool blankets be damned, the man had secrets and for all she knew could be behind the disappearance of the missing ladies. It would pay to be cautious around him.

It would have paid to return the blanket too really, but she couldn't bring herself to, especially when her mother seemed to sleep so comfortably with it on.

Lord Huntingdon snatched the handkerchief from her and strode wordlessly toward a door. Freya paused briefly, taking a moment to eye the grand carved staircase, lined with a plush red carpet. Everything shone and gleamed from the crystal chandelier to the vases on plinths.

"Are you coming?" he demanded, pausing at the door.

"Oh. Yes." She jolted into action and followed him to the door. Gawping wide-mouthed at his wealth was not the best way to start this. How could she take control of the situation if she made him think she'd never witnessed such wealth before?

Which she had. A little. But it never failed to take her by surprise. Were it not for her late birth, her parents would be living in relative comfort, even with her father having to retire from work early but they would never have achieved such wealth, regardless, and now they were all living in genteel poverty. Just one of those vases would probably rescue them from it all. The inequality of it all really did frustrate her.

He pushed open the door and ushered her in. A room lined with bookcases overlooking the rear garden greeted her. She eyed the desk, scattered with papers, and squinted at the scrawled ink but couldn't make out any useful information. A painting hung above the fireplace of a man who looked similar to the earl but not in the eyes.

"Your father?" she asked.

"Yes."

"He was handsome." She grimaced at the words. She had not come here for small talk or to charm the man. Answers were her goal.

"He was a bastard."

She twisted and blinked at him. "Oh. You mean..."

"Not a literal one. Just a generally awful man."

"I—" She fought for a response but failed. "Oh your cheek." Hurrying over, she took the handkerchief from him and pressed him onto the chair behind the desk with one hand. He dropped down with a frown.

Freya dabbed away the fresh blood then flattened the cloth firmly to his face. "I am sorry. Even if you did forget our meeting."

"I didn't forget it deliberately. As I said, I'm a—"

"Busy man," she finished for him. "I know. Though I would not put it past you to have been avoiding me."

"Can you blame me?"

She lifted the cloth then pressed it back down. That stubble covered his jaw again. She concluded it must certainly grow swiftly. "I'm not certain what you mean."

"I do not much relish having my business splashed across newspapers for the rabble to enjoy."

"If you wish to be wealthy, you have to expect people to want to know what you are doing. After all, the *rabble* need something to look forward to in life."

"I hardly chose to be wealthy," he pointed out.

"I should think sacrificing a little privacy is worth all this," she gestured about the room.

"Oh so you think you wouldn't mind having your every move, every heartbreak written about for the general public to consume?"

She lifted a shoulder and tried to ignore the heartbreak part. A strong man like the earl would surely never suffer a real heartbreak. After all, a vaguely attractive man like him could get any woman he wanted. "If I haven't done anything worthy of gossip, why would it matter?"

"So you would not mind someone writing about, oh I don't know, the holes in your coat or how your petticoat is slipping out from underneath your skirts."

Freya's cheeks had to be bright red. They felt as though they were glowing as hot as the embers of a fire. "That's hardly gossip-worthy."

"If you were a countess, it certainly would be."

A burst of laughter escaped her. "A countess? Me? I think the world would turn on its head if that ever happened."

"Still, the idea of being written about made you uncomfortable, did it not?"

"That is entirely beside the point—"

He snatched her wrist and moved her hand away from his face. Though he still wore his thick gloves as did she, the feeling of his fingers around her arm lingered when he released her.

She tilted her lips. "I fear you might scar."

"I shall have to pretend it was from fencing or something far more interesting than an umbrella attack."

Her mouth twitched. "Or a run-in with a fearsome pirate. That's much more manly."

His gaze connected with hers and her chest tightened. His dark eyes searched hers and for the life of her she couldn't look away. What he was looking for, she could not fathom, but so much of her could not help but think these were not the eyes of a man who could harm women. Moments passed and her heart beat hard in her ears.

"I don't like writing gossip," she blurted.

His brows lifted. "Oh."

"That is...I hope to write more serious things. That's why I'm—" She made a vague gesture with her hands.

With a heavy sigh, Lord Huntingdon shoved the other chair out with a foot. "Go on. Sit and ask me your questions, but I doubt I can tell you anything useful."

Chapter Five

WHY WAS HE EVEN HERE? Guy loathed the London parks. They were always overrun with carriages and people and one could hardly stroll through without being mown down by some overeager dandy on horseback. Especially since today was dry, Regent's Park boasted a large number of inhabitants.

If he had any sense, he'd turn on his heel and run.

Apparently, he had none.

Because in the crowds somewhere would be Miss Haversham and her dog. She had told him specifically she walked him here every morning when she'd left his townhouse last night.

He ran a hand over his face and peered about, eyeing each dog walker in search of a small, pale woman with a determined expression.

He knew why he was here really. He'd done a poor job of dissuading Miss Haversham from her search for the missing women. After a sleepless night of analyzing every second of their encounter, he concluded that he had successfully given nothing away about his role in why they had vanished, but he had also not been clever enough to throw her off the trail. Frustrating indeed. There were seldom moments when he could claim to have acted foolishly. Becoming engaged to Amelia might have been one of them—one of the few, however.

But it seemed Miss Haversham had an ability to make his brain function much more slowly and stupidly than usual. Lord knew why. He was no stranger to clever, slightly attractive women, though he had to admit, he knew few with holes in their coats and even fewer who attacked him with umbrellas.

Guy stepped out of the way of a barouche, its occupants bundled up in furs and feathers. Lord, he hated parks. He shouldn't have come. Should not have even thought about seeking her out. It was just going to look—

"Lord Huntingdon?"

He twisted slowly, bracing himself. Which was ridiculous. One didn't need to brace oneself for the sight of a fair-haired lady with a pointed chin and eyes that never looked anything other than shrewd.

His heart gave a strange jolt.

Standing on the opposite side of the path, Miss Haversham eyed him with a lifted brow.

He touched the brim of his hat. "Miss Haversham." He glanced down at the white dog at her heel, its face a muddle of wrinkles and its legs short and stumpy, almost like a bulldog but not quite right. "What manner of dog is that?" he asked before he could stop himself.

A carriage zipped between them. She shrugged. "He's a bulldog," she confirmed. "Sort of anyway. We think he's a mix of some kind."

"To be certain," he muttered.

"Whatever are you doing here, my lord?" she asked, head cocked slightly.

He struggled for an answer. There were a few, after all. Making a fool of himself could be one. Digging himself into deeper trouble with her was another. Or the most realistic answer, what, he had no idea. Now that he had found her, his grand plan of sending her chasing some other story appeared preposterous.

"I thought as the weather was dry..." He gestured vaguely. Several men on horseback passed, making the ground vibrate.

"It is better than yesterday to be certain." She motioned to her face. "How is your cheek?"

"Oh better, thank you." He winced. This was not going as planned. "How is your—"

A procession of carriages moved between them. He despised parks. What could be a better waste of one's time than trying to avoid being run over by those who wished so desperately to be seen? He had far better things to do with his time.

And yet he was here. With her.

Spying a gap in the crowds, he darted across the path to join her, feeling the whip of wind blow past him as someone on horseback rode impatiently by.

"Damned parks," he muttered.

"If you had come here yesterday, it was much quieter."

He glanced at her. "It was pouring rain yesterday."

"Yes, I do recall." Her eyes crinkled with amusement.

Guy cursed inwardly. Why did this woman make him feel like a virginial whelp?

Perhaps because it was not that far from the truth but still, he was no whelp. He had spent much of his life interacting with rich and beautiful women, smart ones too. Some of them likely even more determined than her. Lord knew, plenty of them had been interested in his hand in marriage and had concocted many ridiculous scenarios to spend time with him.

Now he was in his mid-thirties, the eagerness had abated. Of course, it helped he kept away from all but the essential events. It seemed his self-inflicted isolation had roughened his manners and made him forget how to behave around women entirely.

"You really do walk here every day?"

She nodded. "Oh yes. Brig loves to see the people." She paused. "Well, hear the people."

"Sorry?"

"He's practically blind," she told him. "But he loves to be outside and he gets quite tetchy if he does not have a walk every day."

He peered down at the dog who had perched his rear on a patch of grass and seemed quite content with merely sitting there, his tongue lolling out of his mouth. "I see." He frowned. "Brig?"

"He's called The Brigadier really. He was a commanding, severe sort of a puppy so it seemed to suit. But he's very old so I like to do what I can to keep him happy. He deserves it."

He glanced at Miss Haversham, briefly catching the softness in her expression before it was tucked away. He knew why he kept himself hard and unyielding but why did she, he wondered. He almost wished he could relive that moment once more, just so he could see the slight curve of her lips and the steeliness vanish from her gaze.

A few moments passed. She bit her lip and stared at the ground before looking up. "Well, your cheek looks better so that is—"

"Shall we walk together?" he suggested in a rush of words. He'd come here with a plan and damn it, he was going to fulfil it, no matter how awkward and tangled and ridiculous this woman made him feel. Somehow, he needed to keep her away from The Kidnap Club.

OF ALL THE THINGS FREYA had expected to come from Lord Huntingdon, asking her to walk with him was not one of them. Especially after yesterday.

Admittedly, attacking him with an umbrella had not been her finest of moments but he had also made it clear he had no patience for her questions. He had described the last time he'd seen Lady Steele in the vaguest of terms and could tell her little more. She could not help think that if she had seen someone just the day before they had vanished into thin air, she would recall every moment, trying to figure out if there was some clue hidden in the interaction.

Something was still not right about the earl and she would welcome an opportunity to dig deeper.

However, she had certainly not expected that opportunity to be brought so directly to her.

"Shall we?" he pressed, indicating down the slender path that cut through the grass toward The Serpentine. Autumn had left the park an array of greens, browns, yellows and reds. The beddings offered up nothing more than empty patches of dirt.

Yet the park never seemed to get quieter, not until the dead of winter. So it shouldn't mean anything that he was here really. After all, she didn't *own* the park. She could not control who came and visited.

It was still odd, though. That little instinct that had driven her this far through life niggled at her. She couldn't let this be, no matter how she felt about the earl.

Which was almost nothing of course. How could she feel anything else? She scarcely knew the man and dabbing his cheek with a handkerchief and being gifted one of his blankets hardly constituted as a friendship let alone anything else.

Anything else. What was wrong with her? The only way they could be more divided was if he was royalty. He would never understand her life and she would never comprehend his.

"Miss Haversham?" he pressed.

Warmth flooded her cheeks. She must look like she was one step away from the asylum, standing here and contemplating their relationship. Or lack of.

"I cannot," she admitted.

The furrow between his brow deepened "Cannot what? Walk?" He peered down at her. "Are you injured?"

"No, I—"

"I see." His stance stiffened. "Well, I shall leave you—"

"No!" She blew out a breath and tried again, more softly this time. "No, it's just that The Brigadier cannot walk any further." She gestured to the dog. "Once he sits like this, he struggles to get up. I shall have to carry him home now."

He glanced between her and the dog several times. "So you bring him for a walk, but he does not even walk?"

"Well, he manages it a little way here. He's very old," she reminded him.

"And you carry him home?"

She nodded.

"He must weigh a ton."

Freya lifted her chin. "I'm stronger than I look."

"Indeed." He kneeled down and gave the dog a rub under his chin.

She expected that he would bid her good day then. And she couldn't fathom a reason to persuade him to stay. *Oh yes, Lord Huntingdon, why do you not remain here at my side while my blind dog sits on the grass and does absolutely nothing?* But she needed him to stay. Desperately.

For the story of course.

"Perhaps—"

He scooped the dog up in both arms. The Brigadier panted heavily, showing no sign of any unease in the earl's arms.

"What are you—?"

"Which way is home?" the earl asked.

"You really do not need to—"

"He weighs a ton. Are you certain you do this every day?"

Freya gestured along the path that led toward the north gates. "Every day," she confirmed. "He would be frightfully sad if I did not. Are you certain you can manage him?"

"Miss Haversham, I would think you would know better than to question a man's strength, especially when he is in front of a pretty woman."

She blinked several times, glancing around. "Oh. You mean—"

He gave her a sideways look and she bit down on her tongue. For an intrepid reporter, she was being incredibly slow around this man. She could put it down to several things—the great divide between their wealth perhaps or an opening that was vastly different.

Oh, yes, she could not forget that he was keeping secrets of some kind. Of that much, she was certain.

She'd be a fool not to admit, however, that the sight of him hauling her dog around like a fat, white baby touched something inside her. She'd also be a fool if she let it dissuade her from her investigations. For all she knew, he had come here deliberately, to charm her in some way and stop her following this story. Well, it didn't matter if he did look dashing in his winter coat with her dog shedding hairs all over the black fabric. Nothing would stop her from getting her big chance.

"Lord Huntingdon, I cannot help but feel there is something you are not telling me about Lady Steele."

He scowled. "I answered all your questions."

"As vaguely as possible."

"I'm not certain how one can be specific when one knows very little." He hefted the dog in his arms with a grunt, moving the animal so he had a view over the earl's shoulder. "He seems to prefer that."

"Brig wasn't always blind so I think sometimes he pretends he can see."

"Pretends? Dear Lord," he muttered.

"Back to Lady Steele."

"I told you all I know. We, as members of the nobility, tend to run in the same circles. We had a little polite conversation, likely discussed the weather, the health of her family and all that, and went our separate ways. She did not imply she had any intention of vanishing nor that she was in some sort of danger."

"Danger? Do you think she knew she would be kidnapped? That someone would try to harm her?"

"That is not what I said," he said tightly.

"Do you not think these kidnappings strange, though? Does it not concern you? What if it was your mother or...someone else?"

"My mother avoids England at all costs. Too cold apparently." He paused and fixed her with a look. "Unfortunately, the roads are dangerous. They always have been, especially when one is travelling in a luxurious vehicle. Highwaymen have been in existence forever and I'm certain they will remain so."

"So you think these men are taking these women, ransoming them then killing them? Surely it would be easier to return the women?"

"I don't think anything," he insisted. "Because I do not know anything. I am no highwayman but if I were you, Miss Haversham, I would turn my attention away from the kidnappings and back to my gossip columns. If they are willing to kill noble ladies, I'm certain you could end up in danger too."

She pursed her lips. "That sounds like a threat, my lord."

"A warning, Miss Haversham, nothing more. I have no desire to see you harmed. Continue with your gossip column. You're so good at it after all."

"I wish to write this story, my lord."

"Write about balls and the like. I'm certain the gossip columns are far less work than pursuing whatever silly story you think you have here."

Freya held in a heated breath for several seconds She could recall almost every moment she had been told something similar. *You're a woman, Miss Haversham, stick to what you know* or *women simply do not have the capacity to write of the real world* or some word of derision aimed at female writers in general. She had heard it all and each phrase would be forever embedded in her, just like his dismissive words would be.

Releasing the breath and feeling rather like a furious dragon, finally taking care of the knight who had been pestering her for so long, she glared at him. "I am not scared of hard work."

She snatched the dog from his arms and pivoted away from him, taking fast steps along the street to create distance between them.

"I can carry him the rest of the way," he offered while he hurried to catch up.

"No, thank you, Lord Huntingdon. I can manage perfectly well on my own," she called over her shoulder. "Good day."

She could manage the heavy dog perfectly well on her own, just as she would figure out this story on her own too. And if Lord Huntingdon was somehow involved, she'd make certain she would be the first to find out.

Chapter Six

EVERY DAY. MISS HAVERSHAM lugged that bloody heavy dog to the park, there and back, every damned day.

Guy flung aside a dinner invitation and flicked a penknife underneath the wax seal of the next letter, not even taking the time to note the crest as it opened with a satisfying pop of broken wax.

Rubbing his forehead, he squinted at the writing then lowered it to the desk and pushed it aside. He had too much work to do not to mention the duchess's sister to worry about. If he was to help her, they needed to make a move sooner rather than later. With any luck his brother Russell would have some news before long. The man had grown up an orphan and had an uncanny ability to slip through society unnoticed, and no one knew London quite like he did.

So he shouldn't be thinking about a blind old dog.

And the woman who carried him all the time. She'd even mentioned being there in the rain. He could picture it now, her hefting that great lump about while rain seeped through the holes in her coat. There had to be an easier way of keeping the dog happy, surely?

He shook his head to himself and retrieved the discarded letter. All he had to do was read it and *not* think about the dog. Or Miss Haversham. Hardly a challenge considering he'd taken on an earldom at the age of one and twenty and partaken in several kidnappings of high-profile society ladies. This should be a cinch.

Of course, it did not help he'd offended her. He still heard her curt 'good day' and pictured the regal stance of her shoulders as she carted the dog away. How anyone could look regal with such a lummox of a dog in their arms, he did not know, but she managed it.

It was good really. If she stopped pestering him, he would be free to continue aiding these ladies unhindered by a stalking, intrusive reporter.

A light tap at the door brought welcome relief from the jumble that had become his thoughts. "Enter."

Russell ducked into the study, his long length occupying most of the doorway. Russell glanced at the portrait of their father. Guy had discovered mention of his half-brother a while ago, but Marcus Russell hadn't known about it until recently. He had been understandably angry being a self-sufficient sort of a man, but they had come to a decent understanding.

It had to be strange for Russell, though, to have gained a family and a history and frankly, Guy was too busy to push for anything more than they already had. They were never going to be the sort to embrace or share all their innermost secrets and he was happy to keep it that way. Hell, the fewer people who knew the full ins and outs of his life, the better. He couldn't even imagine trying to explain to Russell the real reason Amelia had left him...

"Do you have a moment?" Russell gestured to the scattered pile of letters and documents on his desk.

"Of course." Guy gestured for him to sit.

Russell settled his length into the chair, seeming too long for the thing. Miss Haversham had certainly looked a darn sight more pleasant in it than his brother, fitting almost perfectly against the curved wooden back, her rear nestled into the plush velvet. He scowled. Good God. He'd gone from fat old dogs to salaciously picturing Miss Haversham's rear. He didn't even find her attractive.

Did he?

Guy leaned forward. "You have news?"

"Nothing good." Russell pulled off his gloves and laid them in his lap. "The husband keeps a close eye on his wife. Half the time, it's almost as if she doesn't exist. She doesn't have any friends or family visit, and if he does go out, he leaves her with at least two companions." Russell's lips tightened. "And when I say companions, I mean two brutes who look as though they have had more a chequered background than I have."

"To protect her or to prevent her from escaping?"

"The latter, for certain. I spotted her with them when he left her one day and she looked decidedly uncomfortable."

"She looked well though?"

"As well as a nervous wreck of a woman can."

"So you spoke with her?"

Russell shook his head. "I couldn't get near her, but I know people and I know she's terrified."

Guy hissed out a breath. "Damn it."

"We'll get to her. Somehow."

"Continue following her. I'll figure something out. It certainly seems as though Lady Clearbury's concerns were valid."

Russell nodded gravely. "I've seen too many battered women in my life to miss the signs."

Jaw tight, Guy rubbed a hand over his face. "So have I."

First his mother then his cousin. Would these damned beasts of men never cease? Russell didn't know the extent of their father's behavior, but he had been a bully and entirely happy to lay a hand on Guy's mother when he felt like it. On Guy too at times. He'd been lucky to grow tall and strong quickly enough to put an end to any of that and his mother spent as much time away from home as possible. Russell knew the man was a callous bastard, but he had little idea quite how bad he was.

Then there had been his cousin, who had begged him for help escaping an abusive marriage. Thus The Kidnap Club had been born—helping women flee or hide temporarily without the blame ever being put on them if they were caught. Daisy lived in Ireland now and her husband had given up hope of finding her.

Guy only wished her husband would pay for what he did.

"I'll speak to Lady Clearbury again, see if she has any idea of Lord Pembroke's schedule. Maybe we can engineer some moment alone with Lady Pembroke."

"I'll wait for word from you." Russell rose. "Oh, that Miss Haversham..."

Guy grimaced. Just when he thought he'd forgotten all about her.

"What about her?"

"She's meeting with Rosie this afternoon. Wants to ask her all about her attempted kidnapping."

A harsh curse word nearly escaped him. "And your wife agreed?"

Russell shrugged. "You know Rosie. I can't tell her what to do and I certainly don't intend to start now."

"She could put us all at risk."

Russell fixed him with a stare. "Rosie is entirely capable of handling a reporter and is certain she can send her following some false trail of a story."

He pinched the bridge of his nose. Just when he thought they might be safe from Miss Haversham and her enquiries, the little minx was getting even more involved. "I certainly hope so."

A wide grin spread across his brother's face—one he seldom saw unless he was with his wife. "Trust me. Rosie will put an end to all of this."

LADY ROSAMUNDE RUSSELL sat serenely amongst the chaos of the tearoom, her hands folded neatly in her lap, dark hair coiled high on her head and fixed with an elegant comb that matched her plum-colored dress. Freya pressed a hand briefly to her stomach, actually aware of the holes in the elbow of her coat and how plain and dull she was in comparison. Drawing up her chin, she strode over to the table set with crisp white linen and a delicate tea set.

Mrs. Russell spied her before she reached the table and gave a wave, her smile welcoming. Wonderful. Now Freya felt awful about probing into the kidnapping. No doubt it would have been quite the terrible experience. She lifted her chin and took the last few steps toward the table, skirting a waiter and two pretty young ladies who apparently did not even notice Freya pressing between the tables of the busy room. Largely filled with women at this time of day, the building hosted mostly those from the upper classes, and Freya wished she had been able to choose their meeting place but she could not be picky, not when the former countess had agreed to meet with her with much less persuasion than it had taken to speak with Lord Huntingdon.

"I should have remembered it would be so busy at this time of day." She gestured for Freya to sit and ordered tea for the both of them. "I would have invited you to visit me at home, but we are having the carpets re-laid at present and it is an utter mess."

"I heard you purchased Uppark Place after your marriage," Freya said.

"The house needs a lot of work but it's rather an adventure, so I do not mind."

A young girl brought over the tea, her cheeks rosy and her expression vaguely harried. Freya felt her stomach grumble when a platter of biscuits was set on the table. She had dashed out of the house after walking Brig and there had been no time to eat, but thankfully the chatter in the tearoom ensured no one heard said grumble. She took up a biscuit and nibbled delicately while the girl served the tea. Freya waited until Mrs. Russell had added sugar before following suit.

"I was hoping to ask you about your kidnapping, Mrs. Russell."

"Oh, please call me Rosie." She waved a hand. "Everyone does."

"Oh, of course, um, Rosie." Freya gave a quick smile. She'd dealt with many a lady in her time as the gossip columnist for the chronicle, but the ex-countess already seemed nothing like them. She understood their reservations given she made a living writing of the ins and outs of their lives, so she hadn't anticipated her being quite so welcoming.

"May I call you by your given name?"

Like she could say no. "Yes, of course."

Rosie looked at her, eyes crinkled with amusement. "Which is?"

"Oh!" She set down the biscuit. "Freya."

"It's a pleasure to meet you, Freya. Now to your questions."

"Well, yes..." She tugged a paper and pencil out of her reticule. "I hope you do not mind if I take some notes."

"Not at all but I have little to tell you that is not already known."

"You were taken at gunpoint, yes?"

Rosie nodded, her lips curving as though the memory amused her. "I was indeed."

"By a lone man?"

"Only the one."

"Can you tell me anything about him?"

She lifted a shoulder. "Tall, attractive eyes."

"Attractive?" Freya scowled. What sort of a person would find their kidnapper attractive?

Rosie blinked. "Well, of what I could see, of course. He had a mask." She gestured over her face. "I did not recognize him."

"Did he say anything to you?"

"Just demanded I go with him. When I tried to fight him off, he grabbed me."

"You tried to fight him off?" She glanced over the delicately coiffed woman. She wasn't tiny or delicate, but it wasn't easy to picture this elegant lady fighting off a brutish, world kidnapper. Especially one who, by all accounts, had successfully taken many women.

She glanced around and leaned in. "I keep a knife on me. It's terribly useful. But, unfortunately, he knocked it from my hand and snatched me up!"

"Then what happened?"

"Well, he stuffed me into a carriage but thankfully I was able to escape. I hit my head during the tumble, but I suppose he did not notice I was gone." She lifted her cup to her mouth, took a long sip and watched for Freya's reaction.

"Goodness..." Freya jotted a quick note on her pad. "Did he say anything else to you when he grabbed you?"

"I believe he just cursed at me." Rosie's smiled widened then she swiftly pressed her lips into a line. "Of course it was terribly frightening, but it could have been worse."

"Your aunt said you offered him money, but he refused it."

"I imagine he thought he could get much more by holding me hostage."

"It's odd, though, that he did not return for you after all that effort, do you not think? It's so much risk to take a woman."

"Oh, I kept myself hidden and I suspect he likely realized I am more trouble than I am worth," Rosie said lightly.

"Did he seem the sort to harm a woman?"

"He was a kidnapper!" She pressed a hand to her chest. "A dastardly, awful, frightful kidnapper. I'm sure he would have no concern harming his captive if needs be. I count myself lucky to have escaped."

"No doubt your wits saved you, my lady."

"Rosie," she prompted.

"So that man was certainly alone?"

"Oh yes." She nodded vigorously.

"And he said nothing else?"

"Not a word." She sipped her tea.

"Tell me, what color were his eyes?"

"Blue," she answered swiftly then paused and pressed a finger to her lips. "No. Brown. Certainly brown."

Freya frowned. She found it odd Rosie recalled how attractive the eyes were but not the color. However, if they were really brown, that was the same color as Lord Huntingdon's eyes.

Chapter Seven

HE SHOULDN'T LIKE IT.

Seeing her dart behind a damned tree, that was.

Guy had expected she had given up with her investigations but apparently not. Miss Haversham was back to playing the stalking, nosy reporter, even after Rosie confirmed she had given away no information that would point the finger at them.

His lips twitched as she pressed herself into the trees. He forced his mouth into a straight line. Nothing amused him about her chasing after him, nothing at all, especially when he had been meeting with the duchess. If she figured out their connection, it could be dangerous once they managed to get a hold of Lady Pembroke.

Striding down the steps of the townhouse, he paced over to the black gates of the private park that was encircled by rows of white houses. He paused by the gates, adjusted his gloves and peered up at the patchy blue sky. He heard the rustle of leaves as she tried to remain still and shook his head to himself.

"Miss Haversham..."

He heard a low curse then she eased out from the bushes, a leaf hanging from the brim of her hat. She scowled at it, plucked it off and flung it away. A quick smile crossed her lips, as fake as the heavily corseted waists of the *ton*. Of course, there was no tight corset here, though he couldn't claim to know the layout of Miss Haversham's waist yet. The ugly brown coat with its holes and frayed edges did little to flatter her figure but he suspected she would match up perfectly well to any pretty society lady.

She might even best them. Her porcelain skin and pale, pale hair would certainly be the envy of many a debutante, and now he thought about it, her eyes were rather attractive too, in an odd pale sort of way.

"Lord Huntingdon, what a surprise."

He set her with a look. "Are you really resorting to following me again? I had thought we had put an end to this nonsense."

"You might have thought that but I did not. And I'm not sure how missing women is *nonsense*."

"How is The Brigadier?"

"He's fine, thank you," she said tightly. She glanced toward the duchess's townhouse. "What were you visiting the Duchess of Newhampton for?"

"Good God, woman, hasn't anyone ever told you women should never ask bold questions?"

"Plenty of times," she replied archly. "But a reporter must ask bold questions. It's their job."

Well, that didn't work. He expected her to march off again and leave him standing alone, staring at her back and hoping for her to turn around. Which was about the most preposterous thing he'd ever done. He didn't like women. Didn't need women. Most certainly did not want a certain female reporter in his life. All women spelled trouble.

He could even include his sister-in-law in that. What she knew about lock-picking and knife-wielding and God knows what else most certainly added up to trouble. Luckily, she was Russell's problem.

Miss Haversham, however, was still his.

His problem, that was.

He didn't own her or anything. Most certainly didn't wish to claim any sort of ownership either. Why would he? He'd had enough troubles getting close to sweet women of the *ton*. Amelia had proved to him once and for all he was to remain a bachelor for the rest of his life and he'd made peace with that. The last thing he needed was a troublesome woman like Miss Haversham in his life.

Hell, she'd probably love to write about his...endowment issue in the gossip columns, so putting her off was vital really.

He should just strip naked here and now. That usually worked to frighten women off.

"I know you have no respect for my work, Lord Huntingdon, but I would rather you did not use that patronizing smile on me. It is really rather unbecoming."

He straightened his lips. After all, he certainly could not admit the sardonic smile came from him imagining her reaction to his humiliation.

She smothered a yawn with the back of a gloved hand, and he narrowed his gaze at her. Though the shadows around her eyes were usually dark, they were more defined today, and her eyes a little red. When he followed the movement of her, he noted she trembled.

"Surely you have better things to do than follow me? I should imagine the paper does not pay you handsomely for leaping into bushes."

"The paper will not pay me at all until there is a story—and that is only if they like it."

"So you are standing around, in the cold, utterly exhausted, voluntarily?" He shook his head. "You are completely mad, Miss Haversham."

"I am perfectly sane, and I am not exhaust—" The words were cut off by a yawn.

Jaw tight, he shook his head again and gripped her arm.

"What are you—?"

He led her over to the wrought-iron bench near the entrance of the gardens and forcibly eased her onto it. When she tried to rise, he thrust a finger at her. "Stay."

"But—"

"Stay or I shall haul you over my shoulder, take you home and lock you in a bedroom until you've had rest."

Her mouth opened. "You would not dare." She glanced around. "That's kidnapping."

He offered a slanted smile. "I know."

And little did she know, he was incredibly good at kidnapping.

FREYA SMOTHERED ANOTHER yawn, clamping her teeth together in a bid to hide it. Lord Huntingdon gave her a knowing look and she narrowed her gaze at him.

"Stay here," he ordered, thrusting a steady finger at her.

The fatigue working its way behind her eyelids and throbbing in her temples was the only thing that prevented her from leaping up and storming away. No one told her what to do. She'd been an independent woman for far too long to listen to orders from him.

But so many nights working late with Lucy plus finishing up her column *and* devoting the rest of her time to delving into this story had taken its toll. If he snatched her up, she wouldn't have the strength to fight him and she'd already embarrassed herself with that blasted umbrella and scoring a mark across his face that still lingered. She didn't want to add being hauled over his shoulder like a flour sack or collapsing at his feet to the list at this point.

He strode out of the gates and Freya peered around at the empty park. Where was he even going? Why was she not using her chance to dart off?

It had to be down to the tiredness, that was all. Or, of course, her curiosity as to why he had been visiting the duchess. It could be an innocent visit of course, but in her time covering the upper echelons of society, she had seldom found many of their furtive actions to be innocent.

Which meant he could be having an affair with her.

That had already crossed her mind with regards to the missing Lady Steele, but she hadn't really wanted to consider it, though she could not quite fathom why. If handsome looks, a strange sort of charm, broad shoulders and a stern gaze that made one's chest tighten wasn't a prime candidate for the sort of man who sleep with other people's wives, what did? She would have to face facts. Lord Huntingdon had been a bachelor since his broken engagement and he was a man, after all. He must have needs. He could well be indulging those needs with the married women of the *ton*.

A little knot bunched in her throat. She couldn't fathom why it was so hard to admit.

Perhaps because he had given her a blanket, and carried her dog, and was now walking toward her with a crumpet in hand. Convincing herself this man could be responsible for missing women and scandalous affairs was growing harder by the second.

He thrust the crumpet at her, the warm-buttered scent making her stomach growl.

"Here, eat."

She took it, clasping it by the paper wrapper, and peered up at him. "What's this?"

"A crumpet." He seated himself on the bench beside her.

"I know what a crumpet is, but why?"

He fixed her with a look. "You are exhausted, and no doubt have barely had time to stop to eat."

How could he even know that about her? She glanced at the buttery treat and sighed. She couldn't resist this anymore than she could a good story. Maybe this was like eating the forbidden apple, but she didn't see what else she could do. Freya hadn't eaten all day, and it would be rude to turn it down.

Even if he could be an affair-having rake who had somehow become involved in the kidnapping of women. She licked a drop of butter from the crumpet and barely masked a moan.

Lord Huntingdon's expression became strangely pained and he turned away to eye the gardens. Freya used the opportunity to lap up every crumb, eating as though she had never eaten food before. When she crumpled up the paper and stuffed it in her coat pocket, he finally looked at her

"Better?"

She nodded. "Thank you."

"You need to look after yourself better. Do you not have anyone at home making sure you eat and sleep?"

"You're not my mother, Lord Huntingdon."

"Your mother should be ensuring you eat."

She stiffened. "I am eight and twenty, my lord. Does your mother still ensure you eat?"

His lips curved. "She writes and asks me if I'm eating well. Does that count?"

"Hardly. Besides, my mother is in no fit state to look after me at present."

"Ah. I'm sorry to hear that."

She eyed him. He wasn't lying. Concern flickered on his brow. It only added to her confusion. Who was this man who cared if she was cold and wanted to see her fed and rested? Why should an earl even care about someone like her? She was nothing more than an annoyance, a fleck of fluff on his shoulder or a spot of dirt on his shoes. She'd met enough titled gentlemen to know that even a woman in genteel poverty meant nothing to them, especially if she was not beautiful and willing to sell her body.

"What is wrong with your mother?" he asked.

"She's been ill for a while," she admitted. "She cannot seem to get over what ails her, and unfortunately my father is old and suffers ill health too, so I cannot rely on him to look after her."

His gaze took on an odd quality. Almost like…admiration. "So you look after your parents as well as spending your time hiding in bushes?"

"I wasn't hiding," she protested.

He cocked his head. "You must like trees very much indeed then." He reached forward, his body coming in toward hers. For one odd moment, she thought he might kiss her. His gaze moved to her lips then up to her hair and her heart did a strange leap into her throat. She tried to swallow it back down but could not bring herself to even move.

What would she do if he did kiss her? Leap up? Slap him perhaps? Or just let it happen and see what it would be like to kiss an attractive earl with a dark brow and shoulders that begged for her to curl her hands up them?

Lord Huntingdon pulled his hand away and moved back then waved a brown leaf in front of her. "Evidence," he said, his grin wry. "You were hiding in that tree."

Freya blew out a long breath. Yes, it was. Evidence of her utter ridiculousness. She needed to be much more on guard around this man.

Chapter Eight

GOOD DAY, MISS HAVERSHAM.

How hard was that to say? Give her the crumpet, ensure she's eaten then be on his way. The less time spent around her, the better. Especially when she had still not given up following him.

Oh yes, most especially when he could kill to kiss her.

It had been a vicious combination of how suddenly delicate she had seemed plus the way she licked butter from her lips and those wide eyes surrounded by fair lashes. He'd always been one to fall for a woman in need, and despite her bold determination, one would be a fool not to notice that Miss Haversham was in need.

Hell, not only did she have a blind old dog, she also had ailing parents and apparently went without food and sleep. Ever since he'd been a boy it had been in him to play rescuer, and despite his vows to keep away from women, he couldn't resist this sort of call.

Of course, if he stayed with her, perhaps he could persuade her away from the story again…

Yes, that was a far better reason for him to stay than wanting to rescue her or, God forbid, kiss her. He peered around the park. At least there was no one here but he couldn't think what had come over him, wishing to kiss this pesky reporter in public.

Or wishing to kiss her at all.

Because kisses led to more, and he could not offer more. *Would not* offer more. Once he got her to the bedroom, she'd see the truth of his problems and there would be hell to pay. Really, he should not even be assuming a woman like Miss Haversham would consider joining him in the bedroom, but his unruly bloody mind would not cease going there. She'd be pale against his red bedding though the outline of her was a little fuzzy. Who knew what sort of a figure lay under that oversized coat? Was she lithe or curvaceous? He wagered more on the lithe side considering she hardly ate but who could tell under that sack of a garment?

And why was he wasting his time entertaining such thoughts?

"Are you feeling better?"

She glanced down at her hands before looking up. "Yes," she admitted.

He knew the admission cost her. Miss Haversham was the sort of woman who ploughed on through, regardless of how tired or hungry she was. It didn't take being an investigative journalist to figure that much out about her.

While it made her a royal pain in his behind, he could not help admire such a trait. Since inheriting his title, he couldn't think of a day when he had not had some sort of work to do. He found those who enjoyed leisure time or didn't throw themselves into work hard to understand. If one has a duty, one should do it.

It seemed Miss Haversham had several duties, but he wished she didn't feel she had one to this story. If she figured anything out, there'd be hell to pay.

But she wouldn't. All of these years doing this, and no one had figured them out. Not to mention, he was as cautious as they could come. There was no denying her tenacity but coming upon the idea of him partaking in kidnappings was a stretch for anyone, even someone as clever as her.

"You really should cease following me, Miss Haversham. It appears to be tiring you out."

"You are hiding something, Lord Huntingdon, and I intend to find out what it is."

"I was not aware visiting with a friend was some illicit deed."

A pale brow arched. "It can be if that friend is a certain sort."

A laugh escaped him. He'd never even had *that* sort of a friend. Amelia had been the closest to that happening and she'd near sprinted from him when she had seen the size of him. Not that it had shocked him, but he'd rather hoped seeing as they loved each other, they might be able to figure something out. Of course, he could have waited until they were wed, and she had no choice but to do the deed, but he had more respect for the both of them than to do that.

She peered at him. "The duchess is an attractive woman. I do not see how that's amusing."

"The duchess has no more interest in me than I do her."

"What of Lady Steele? She was beautiful and accomplished. You could have been having an affair with her."

"It takes more than mere beauty and accomplishment to capture my attention."

"Oh? Like what?"

"Like..." He frowned, trying to recall exactly why he had fallen for Amelia in the first place. She'd been funny and rather vivacious, he supposed. Almost the opposite of him in some ways. Though he still resented their broken engagement and the humiliation that had come with her behavior, he struggled to picture how they would have functioned together these days. "Like courage, and tenacity. A sense of hard work."

She opened her mouth then closed it. Damn it. He'd just described her, had he not? And she likely well knew it.

"And dark hair," he added. "Lots of curves. Voluptuous."

Her gaze narrowed to slits. "Of course."

"Anyway, I am not having an affair so you can keep that out of your column, Miss Haversham, unless you take pleasure in ruining lives."

"I do not take pleasure in ruining lives," Miss Haversham protested. "But it was the only job open to a woman."

"Why not find another job if you do not enjoy doing it?"

"Spoken like a true noble. Of course you would not understand having to work without pleasure to survive."

"I understand full well working without pleasure. Most of my duties seldom bring me pleasure, but if I did not do them, my estates would not survive and the people who rely on me to keep them running would flounder."

She blinked a few times. "Oh. Well, I..." She lifted her chin, bright spots of color on her cheeks. "Well, you will never go hungry."

"That is true," he conceded. "And that is where we are different, I suppose."

DIFFERENT. YES. ENTIRELY different. So why was Freya struggling to remember that? He had wealth, privilege, education.

Good looks.

She had none of those. Everything she had was fought for and it still wasn't enough. But if this story broke...

No, *when* this story broke and she found out what had happened to those women, she would finally be recognized as a reporter of note. The newspaper couldn't turn down any of her future articles after that, surely?

"Perhaps it might be best if you turn your attention to another story," Lord Huntingdon suggested. "Surely there is something else you can write about that does not involve you hiding in trees and following me about?"

"Well, you would like that, would you not? Especially if you were guilty."

His brows lifted. "You think me involved in their disappearance?"

"Well..." She pressed her lips together. Wonderful, now she had put herself in thoroughly hot water, practically assuming a peer of the realm of kidnap.

That wasn't exactly what she was saying but he had to be hiding something. "Why else would you be so insistent I drop the story?"

"Perhaps because I'm getting a little tired of having my every move watched, not to mention you are so exhausted you haven't noticed that half of your hair has spilled free and that your coat buttons are done up wrong."

"Oh." She put a hand to her hair and felt a long spiral of it trailing down the back of her coat. Then she glanced at her buttons and grimaced. If her plan today had been to make an utter fool of herself, she was doing a fine job of it.

"If it's any consolation, your hair is quite lovely."

Freya rose sharply from the bench. "I do not need your patronizing compliments, my lord." Especially about the one thing she actually took pride in.

He held up both hands. "I promise there was nothing patronizing about it."

"Well...I..."

She twisted and released a sound of frustration then stomped off toward a small pond at the center of the gardens. A few ducks bobbed on the surface and she rather envied them, sitting around, all unflustered and entirely sure of what they needed to do, which was, well, behave like a duck she supposed.

Her plans for today had gone entirely awry. She had hoped she might spot something sinister or scandalous but all she'd found out was that Lord Huntingdon noticed *everything* and they were more alike than she'd like to admit.

Footsteps sounded behind her, so she picked up the pace, following the circular path around the pond. She focused on the iron gates. Perhaps if she moved quickly enough, she could slip through and slam the gates on him and put an end to this humiliation.

Not that running away from an earl would be the most dignified of moments but how much longer could she tolerate being in his presence before she did or said something silly?

"Miss Haversham," he called.

She ignored him.

"Miss Haversham," he repeated, his voice firm. A hand curled around her wrist, tugging her to a halt. She twisted but he was closer than she'd anticipated so she pressed her palms to his chest to get some distance.

He wavered for a moment and she frowned, glanced down and spotted the heels of his polished hessians too close to the edge of the pond. She grabbed for him too late. He toppled backward, his eyes going wide before he vanished into the murky water.

Frozen, she eyed the water, the ripples sending the ducks bobbing about aggressively. It couldn't be that deep so he wouldn't drown.

Would he?

"Oh Lord." Scanning the surface, she tried to swallow the knot in her throat. With a shake of her head, she flicked open the buttons of her coat and shoved off her boots with each foot to the heel. "Jumping into a pond in the middle of Autumn. Just wonderful," she muttered before taking a leap.

The water closed about her, stealing the breath from her lungs. She gasped when it reached her neck. "Whoever created this pond was an imbecile."

Why would anyone make one so deep? She fumbled around where she'd last seen the earl, aware of the mud seeping between her toes. Her fingers brushed fabric and she snatched it, hauling with all her strength until the earl emerged, his eyes closed. She shoved him toward the edge of the pond then clambered out.

Teeth chattering, she cursed under her breath and paced around then grabbed the collar of his coat then dragged him fully from the water. He weighed a ton and she supposed he had been weighted down by his clothes when he had gone under.

His eyes remained closed. Panic fluttered in her chest. The park remained empty with no sign of a strong man to help revive him or some tender woman who would know what to do with him. She kneeled beside him and prodded his chest.

"Um, Lord Huntingdon." His dark lashes stayed fanned across his cheeks. His hat was long gone, and his damp hair curled outrageously. She wanted to touch it, which was entirely ridiculous given he was knocked senseless. She poked him again, and when he didn't respond she poked him several more times.

"Oh God, I've killed an earl," she wailed, dropping her head to his chest.

"I'm not dead."

She lifted her head swiftly.

He cracked an eye and peered at her. "Though there's something vaguely celestial about all this." He motioned to her loose, wet hair that spilled about her shoulders.

"Oh thank goodness!" Freya flung herself forward, looping her arms around his neck. Her lips met his in a rush and she stilled briefly, her eyes likely about as wide as his.

Then an arm wrapped about her waist and he kissed her back. She closed her eyes, lost to the sensation of his cold lips combined with his warm mouth. He kissed her hard, fiercely. Like he hadn't kissed a woman in an age. Like a man who had nearly died, she supposed. He ran his hands up and down her back and a shiver wracked her.

He put his hands to her arms and eased her away. "You're cold."

"No." She sucked in a heated breath and tried to tamp down on the disappointment creating a cold swirl in her stomach. "I mean I am but—"

But what? The shiver was nothing to do with her plunge into the water? She could hardly admit that.

"We should get you home and dry," he said with a glance around. "And we should certainly move before someone happens upon us."

She nodded, fingering a wet strand of hair. "Yes. We should. Of course." She offered a swift smile. "Sorry for the whole, um, pond thing."

He sat and pressed a finger to the back of his head. "I knocked my head when I went under I think."

"I really did nearly kill you then."

Lifting a shoulder, he offered her a lopsided smile that warmed her from her toes to her head. "I might have deserved it." He stood and offered her a hand up. "I don't suppose you wish to retrieve my hat, do you?"

She followed her gaze to spot it floating alongside the ducks. "Unfortunately, I think the ducks have claimed it as their own."

"Alas, I think you might be right." He bent to retrieve her coat and offered it out to her.

She grabbed it from him, threw it about her shoulders and took her offered boots too. "I had better be going, my lord," she said, turning with her boots in hand. "Lots to do. A dog to walk. Articles to write. You know how it is."

"Miss Haversham…"

She hastened down the path with bare feet and slipped out of the gates. Her bare feet and sodden state garnered looks from pedestrians and a gentleman even paused to ask if she needed help. Freya waved away his offer with a smile and didn't stop until she was certain Lord Huntingdon hadn't followed her. Pressing her back against the brick of a small butcher's shop, she waited for her breaths to slow before slipping on her boots and doing her coat up properly.

She put a hand to her lips. What on earth had she just done?

Chapter Nine

A FITTING FOR HIS NEWEST jacket should be dull enough for a man to take his mind off a kiss.

Should be.

But was not.

Guy stared straight ahead out of the window of the tiny shop, potentially waiting as the seamstress tutted and tugged and moved around him.

"I must thank you for visiting me here, Lord Huntingdon," Miss Walker said as she did another loop around him, paused, rubbed her chin and plucked something from the front of the coat. "I did not want to make you wait any longer."

"Your services are quite in demand." He glanced down at the jacket and tugged the edges. "I know why. You do excellent work."

Miss Walker clasped her hands together and beamed at him. "Thank you, my lord, it means a lot to me to hear that."

He eyed the seamstress. Around Miss Haversham's age with tightly coiled dark hair pulled into a severe bun, and generous, pretty lips, Miss Walker had garnered herself quite the reputation with members of the *ton* lately. He didn't much care for fashions but he enjoyed a perfectly fitted jacket.

TAKING THE SPINSTER 77

And he needed one now. His dip in the pond had likely rendered those garments entirely unusable. He'd overheard his housekeeper speaking with Brown about the matter and how furious the laundry maids had been.

Brown hadn't even lifted a brow when Guy had arrived home, drenched from head to toe, and Guy refused to offer an explanation regardless. What could he say? He'd decided to take a little swim? He'd fallen into a pond then been rescued by a nymph who kissed him as though she needed his kiss more than anything in the world?

"Lord Huntingdon, are you displeased?"

He blinked and focused his attention back on Miss Walker. "Not at all."

"You had a strange sort of look then." She pursed her lips and eyed the jacket critically. "A minor adjustment to the sleeves I think. I can do that right now."

"Of course." He swallowed hard and forced away thoughts of wet gowns and small waists and generous hips and long, *long* wet hair.

And how she tasted...

The bell at the door rang and Guy looked up, grateful for the interruption.

That was, until *she* walked in.

"Lucy, I—" Miss Haversham's gaze met his. "What are *you* doing here?"

"What am I doing here? What are you doing here?" he demanded. "Is it not enough that you follow me everywhere else? Can I not have a moment's peace?" His words came out sharper than intended, mostly because he'd been recalling the exact flavor of her mouth and how soft she'd felt against him. Now he suspected he must have conjured her somehow, just to ensure the torture was complete.

"Actually, I—"

"Miss Walker, I apologize, but Miss Haversham has been following me because she has some odd idea that I am involved in a story."

Miss Walker lifted a hand. "Oh, Lord Huntingdon—"

"Miss Haversham, I suggest you leave. With haste."

Her mouth tightened and she shucked off that awful coat, flinging it over the long table that ran along the front of the shop then added her hat to the pile. "I am here for Miss Walker," she snapped. "Your ego might have you believe a woman cannot have a life outside of you, my lord, but Miss Walker is my friend. I had no idea you were going to be here."

He looked to Miss Walker.

She nodded, biting down on her lip. "It is true, my lord. Freya helps me when I have more orders than I can manage. We have known each other since I moved to England as a child."

"Ah." He drew in a deep breath.

One kiss and he'd become an utter fool. Miss Haversham had turned him into a madman. He blew out a long breath. "I apologize—"

"I can see you're busy, Lucy, so I shall leave you to it," Miss Haversham said, making a grab for her coat.

"Oh, you can help me if you do not mind," Miss Walker suggested. "I only need to do the sleeves, but I could use an extra hand."

Freya glanced between them both and shoulders sagged. "Of course."

Guy froze as she neared him. Miss Walker directed her to pinch the fabric and he fixed his gaze on the street outside, the movement of people slightly blurry through the thick, beveled glass.

In the peripheral of his vision, Miss Haversham remained perfectly still, her gaze cast down while Miss Walker worked. He stole a few glances, liking the way her pale lashes fanned against her cheeks far too much and wondering how she gathered all that hair so with one simple comb.

It had been spectacularly long when wet but how would it look unleashed? He never thought a blasted comb could be a temptation. Given he had managed to resist the lure of any woman since Amelia, he would have thought himself impervious to such thoughts.

But, no, this wretched comb taunted him. One little tug and her hair would spill down her shoulders and wind down to just above her rear. It would swing there, begging for his touch. Then once he'd run the length of her hair through his fingers, he'd curve his hands over that arse and cup her close.

And she would panic and flee, just like Amelia had done. Except it would be even worse. He'd likely end up in the gossip columns.

He swallowed hard and eyed a smudge on the window. Forget the kiss, forget her hair, forget ever touching her. How hard could that be?

LUCY SHUT THE DOOR behind Lord Huntingdon and she and Freya froze until the blur of him had passed the window. Lucy pivoted on a heel and hastened over, grasping Freya's hands. "I did not know you knew the Earl of Henleigh."

"What was he even doing here?" Freya asked, finally releasing the breath that she suspected she had been holding since she first stepped into Lucy's shop.

"He offered to come here for the final fitting, can you believe it?" Lucy shook her head. "He is such a gentleman."

"Well, I suppose he's not terrible," she murmured.

"What sort of story are you doing on him? Something to do with one of his lovers I would wager." She waggled her brows.

Freya sank onto a spindly chair. How her legs had held her up for so long, she did not know. Seeing the earl after kissing him only yesterday had made her legs feel as though they were skinnier and weaker than the legs of the furniture beneath her.

"I do not think he has any lovers."

Lucy scowled and drew out the second chair then sat opposite. "An attractive rich man like that? He must have women clamoring to be his countess."

Freya didn't want to think on that. She eyed the woodgrain of the table and traced the pattern with a finger. "He's not that handsome."

"Either he has done something truly awful or you are as blind as your dog, Freya. I see plenty of handsome nobles in my job and that man is one of the most handsome."

"Well, if you like that sort, he is acceptable I suppose," she muttered.

"Acceptable?" Lucy leaned in and peered at Freya. "I think you have been working too hard. I shall certainly have to hire someone else now."

"No!" Freya snapped her head up. "You cannot afford it."

"I will be able to soon. Just a little while longer. But if it is taking that much toll on you, I will refuse your help."

Freya shook her head vigorously. She could not bear the thought of Lucy delaying her dreams. Just a little more money and she would be able to have a new shop and someone to assist her. Hopefully if Freya could keep her wits about her, they would both be on the rise up together. How wonderful it would be.

"I wish to keep helping you," she assured Lucy. "I just do not like the earl much."

Which was true. Was it not? After all, he had scolded her for simply visiting her friend and derided her writing. Just because his kisses were pleasant and his body made her stomach do funny little twirls, did not mean she liked the man.

"He's a little stiff sometimes but seems pleasant. Will you tell me what this story is?"

Pleasant? There was that word again. It was too insipid, too mild to describe that kiss, even if she wished to keep it that way. Scorching, mind-numbing, transformative...any and all of those words worked far better.

"I believe he knows something about the disappearance of these noble women."

"But what could he possibly know?"

"I'm not certain." She sighed. "He evades my questions, but he was seen with one of them before she vanished, *and* his new sister was kidnapped shortly before her marriage to his brother. Apparently, she fought off the kidnapper."

"Goodness, how did she fight him off?"

"The story is she attacked him with a knife." Freya shrugged. "How many countesses do you know who could fight a man off with a knife?"

Lucy lifted her shoulders. "Certainly none of the ones I make dresses for."

"The whole thing is odd, and I swear Lord Huntingdon knows *something*."

"So you've been following him?"

Freya's cheeks warmed. "I did not intend to get caught."

"Caught by an earl, how exciting."

"It was not exciting." Freya stabbed a tiny floating piece of fluff to the table with one finger while her stomach gave a traitorous twirl at the memory of Lord Huntingdon's lips against hers. "Not exciting at all."

"He seemed rather contrite after giving you an earful. Perhaps he shall answer your questions now."

"Doubtful," Freya muttered. "The man is not being cooperative at all."

"Rather like someone else I know," Lucy said with a smile.

"Oh, Lucy, why can this not be easy? I know I have a story here and I know if I can find out what has happened to these women, this will make my career. No more silly gossip and no more men looking down their nose at me because I write about nobles bedding one another. If only I had not—" She clamped her mouth shut.

"Had not...?"

The temptation to tell Lucy burned on her tongue. To confess all about the kiss and how it distracted her, how it confused her to no end.

How it made her hungry for more.

She swallowed the admission. What a fool she would sound if she admitted they had kissed let alone the fact she wanted it to happen again. Goodness, even her closest friend would be hard pressed to believe an earl had kissed her no matter how much Lucy loved her. She was plain, poor and trying to write a story about him. Nothing about that made them a perfect match.

Freya flicked away the piece of fluff and fixed a smile upon her face. "I just regret not being firmer with him."

"Well, I know you, Freya, and peer of the realm or not, you will get the answers you want."

"I hope you are right."

"When am I not?"

Freya rolled her eyes and gave her a nudge with her shoulder. "Never, of course."

"That means I'm not wrong about the earl being handsome either."

Freya struggled to argue with Lucy on that.

Chapter Ten

GUY COULDN'T FATHOM quite who was following who at this point. Regardless, he couldn't help smile when he spotted Miss Haversham and Brig. The dog had perched himself on the path and apparently had no inclination to budge, his rear firmly planted while Miss Haversham tugged on his lead. He couldn't hear her pleading with the dog, but he saw her mouthing something like *damned dog* as she motioned down the path.

He followed her gaze to spy a man on horseback riding recklessly along the path, caring little for those in his way. Several people had to practically jump out of his way. He swung his gaze back to the dog and Miss Haversham. He already knew what she planned to do, the bloody foolish woman.

Before she darted forward, he raced over. The ground vibrated beneath him, the sound of the hooves hammering in his ears. He looped his arms around the dog, vaguely heard a feminine scream and rolled onto the grass as a woosh of air rushed past him.

Brig wriggled in his arms while Guy gathered his breath. He winced and released the dog as Miss Haversham rushed to his side. "Lord Huntingdon, you could have been killed!"

"The second time this week," he murmured.

The woman was a menace. He'd never had a brush with death until meeting her, though he might have exaggerated his injuries upon falling into the lake. The truth was, he'd rather enjoyed her concern over him.

He eased himself from the ground, waved away her offered hand and brushed the grass from his jacket. He looked in the direction of the rider, but Guy suspected the chap hadn't even noticed the dog or his unexpected acrobatics. He winced and pressed a hand to the back of his neck. He was too old for this nonsense.

"Are you hurt?"

The concern in her gaze did something odd to his insides as though they had suddenly turned to liquid. He should not like it, but he was hugely tempted to feign injury and see if he could persuade her to assist him home. Then he could invite her in and have her tend to him and—

No. He had come to apologize. Nothing more. Not repeat the kiss. Not have her touch him. Not feel her body against his. All those things would lead to him wanting more and he simply couldn't have more. He had resigned himself to that fact. He'd remain a virgin forever thanks to his ridiculous size and he'd made his peace with that after Amelia.

"I'm well."

She put a hand to his arm, and he bit back a groan. If he didn't stop acting like a damned virgin, he'd be in trouble. The mere touch of a hand to his arm shouldn't have any sort of impact upon him. But, then, maybe it was more to do with the owner of the hand. So much of him wished to see her like he had seen her at the pond, with ridiculously long hair in wet ringlets trailing down her waist and her dress clinging to a small waist and quite generous hips.

"Oh. Your coat." She touched the seam and prodded a finger through. He flinched when she connected with his side.

"Well, that's not going to help," he grumbled.

"That's not your new one, is it?"

"Yes," he said tightly.

"Oh no. I'm so, so sorry."

He eyed the dog who sat placidly on the grass, his tongue lolling out the side of his mouth. He envied Brig somewhat. It must be nice to be so oblivious. "I take it he is done for the day."

"We scarcely walked unfortunately but we actually have sunshine today. I couldn't let him miss out on that."

"So you carried him here?"

She kicked a few blades of grass. "Only most of the way."

"Good God, woman."

Miss Haversham's eyes widened. "What?"

He shook his head, unable to utter what he was thinking. She was either the daftest woman he'd ever met or the kindest. Maybe a combination of both. Underneath that determined exterior, beat the soft heart of a woman who helped out at her friend's business and looked after sick parents and carried her dog to the park and back every day.

He couldn't help wonder if there might be room in there for him, somehow.

Preposterous. He needed this to end. Now. Send her on her way, never risk humiliating himself in front of a woman ever again and ensure the secrecy of The Kidnap Club remained.

He waved a hand. "I just came to apologize."

"Oh?"

"For yesterday. I made an assumption and I was wrong."

"I really didn't know you were going to be there, my lord."

He nodded. "I realize that. That's why I sought you out."

"I see."

"I am sorry for accusing you. You might understand why, though."

Miss Haversham lifted her chin. "I cannot imagine what you mean."

"So hiding in bushes and standing in muddy puddles brings nothing to mind?"

Her lips quirked a little. "I am afraid you are talking in riddles, my lord."

Christ, the woman was bold. And fool that he was, he liked it.

A little furrow appeared between her brows and she shifted slightly, ducking behind him. He frowned. "What on earth...?"

She gripped his arms. "Do not move," she ordered, her knees bent so she crouched low.

"But—"

"Blast," she muttered. She lifted a hand and waved to someone behind him.

Guy twisted to view a fashionably dressed gentleman making his way over to them. He tipped his hat to Miss Haversham while Guy eyed him closely. His garments were well made but a little gaudy for his tastes. The word dandy came to mind. Sandy-colored hair curved down the sides of his face and Guy suspected the man had little problems garnering the attention of women.

But did he garner Miss Haversham's attention?

He glanced back at her. She smiled generously and dipped her head in greeting to the man.

Guy hated him.

FREYA'S CHEEKS HURT already from the false smile. She loathed Simeon Curtis. The man pretended to be lovely to her, but she knew he had tried to persuade the editor to rid the newspaper of her. She'd overheard him complaining of the London Chronicle becoming some fluffy feminine newspaper, despite the fact that many had gossip columns, and while she did not enjoy writing the column, she was darn good at it. Not to mention, several newspapers had women writing for them—usually under pseudonyms—but they were still popular. Simeon hated women unless they were in his bed and thought himself utterly superior to the opposite sex.

"Will you not introduce me?"

Freya sucked in a breath at his boldness but conceded. The best way to deal with men like Simeon was to be polite but cold and send him on his way. If she argued with him or pointed out his flaws, he went into flat denial and somehow made her look like the bad person. "Forgive me. Lord Huntingdon, this is Mr. Simeon Curtis. He writes for the London Chronicle." She gestured to Simeon. "And this is Lord Huntingdon, the Earl of Henleigh."

Simeon bowed deeply. "I thought I recognized you, my lord. Please do not tell me Freya has taken to pestering you directly for her column?"

"Not at all," Lord Huntingdon said stiffly.

Freya ground her jaw at the use of her first name.

"If it were up to me, we wouldn't even have that column."

"I am sure Lord Huntingdon would agree with you, *Simeon*, but we must give the readers what they want. I cannot recall how many letters I have had in the past week about it." She pressed a finger to her lips. "A few more than you I imagine."

Simeon's lips flattened into a straight line, and Freya regretted her words. She refused to be intimidated by him, but she did not have the time to be making enemies at the newspaper and bickering with silly little men was beyond her.

Usually.

Usually he did not try to make a fool of her in front of the earl.

"Men do not have the time to waste writing letters, unfortunately, or else I should have received a lot more," Simeon muttered.

"What was your most recent story, Mr. Curtis?" Lord Huntingdon enquired.

He lifted his chin, looking straight down his nose at the earl. Freya nearly shook her head at his boldness.

"A piece on marine insurance and what an investment it shall be."

"Oh yes. I believe I cast my gaze over it. I cannot really recall the content, though, I am afraid."

Simeon's cheeks reddened slightly but he recovered swiftly. "I am certain many of my stories would be of interest to you, my lord. Perhaps you will allow me to send them to you?"

"I rather think not. I hardly have any leisure time, what with being an earl and all that. You know how it is."

Freya bit the inside of her cheek to prevent herself from laughing aloud. Simeon looked as though he might explode, the veins in his neck growing stark and the redness spreading downward and vanishing underneath his cravat.

"Of course, of course." He gestured to Freya. "No doubt Freya is taking up much of your time too. Perhaps you would like to join me for a walk?" He offered her an arm. "We can leave Lord Huntingdon to his busy schedule then."

"I am afraid she is accompanying me." Lord Huntingdon held out his arm.

She skipped her gaze between the two of them. What was happening here?

"Miss Haversham?" Simeon prompted.

She jerked into action, taking Lord Huntingdon's arm. "Forgive me, Simeon, but the earl and I are incredibly busy. Good luck with your latest little story." She smiled sweetly.

Simeon's nostrils flared then he straightened his shoulders and tipped his hat. "Good day to you both."

Lord Huntingdon did not bother responding and led her away with a tug at her arm. Thankfully Brig understood their need to escape and ambled along beside them until they reached a bridge that crossed the river. Freya loosened her arm from the earl's. "I think we can stop now. He's most certainly not following us."

"I rather thought we were taking a walk." He gestured to the path over the other side of the river.

"I thought we were escaping Mr. Curtis."

A dark brow rose. "Did you wish to escape him?"

"Of course! The man is insufferable."

"He was flirting with you."

"Flirting?"

"Yes, it's something men do when they like a woman," he intoned.

"I understand what flirting is, but Simeon was not flirting with me."

"No? So all that Freya business." He mimicked Simeon's tones. "And offering to walk with you?"

"In case you did not notice, he derided my writing and suggested I should not be working at the newspaper at all."

He scowled. "Did he?"

"Yes!" She shook her head. How on earth did he misconstrue all of that for flirting? "He only calls me Freya because he likes to demean me, and he was hoping you would gladly send me on my way."

"I did not like it one jot," he muttered.

"Neither did I."

"The man is an ass."

She nodded. "Thank you for not sending me off with him, by the way."

"I would not trust him with my spinster aunt."

"Well, I do not suppose I would either."

He gave her a look. "Aunt Edith has survived three husbands."

"He's quite insufferable but not immortal, Lord Huntingdon."

"If he calls you Freya again, I shall gladly call him out."

"Goodness, that's a little extreme."

His scowl deepened. "Men like that need to be taught a lesson."

"I should think being dismissed by the Earl of Henleigh was enough. He doesn't need a bullet hole in his chest too."

He sighed and offered her his arm again. "Does it make up for yesterday at least?"

"You humiliating Simeon in exchange for your false accusations?" She pretended to ponder the matter. "I suppose so."

Freya hesitated taking his arm but only briefly. She should not really. Far better for her to still be annoyed at him and focus on her story. But he had come to her rescue twice today so she could hardly deny him. She took his arm and tried not to think about how pleasant it was to be strolling around the park on the arm of this handsome gentleman.

Tried and utterly, utterly failed.

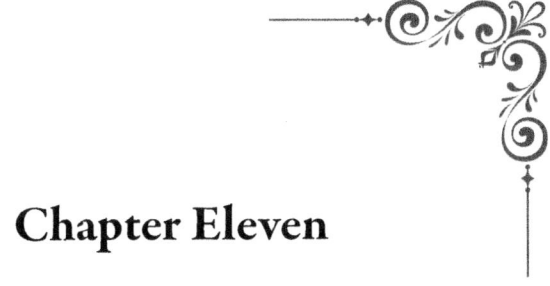

Chapter Eleven

"YOU REALLY RESCUED Freya's dog?" The seamstress shook her head, her lips curving while she shoved pins into the seam of his coat.

"Well, I could hardly leave the thing to be run over now, could I?"

"At the expense of my work," Miss Walker muttered, amusement tinging her voice. "Was it worth it?"

Worth it? Hell, Guy suspected he'd be happy to ruin every article of clothing he owned just to save Miss Haversham hurt. "Just," he murmured rather than admitting it aloud.

"She walks that dog every day, come rain or shine," Miss Walker said past the pins in her mouth. "Lift your arm please," she ordered.

Guy did as he was told, feeling her tug and pull at the side of the coat. It could have waited, he supposed, but he knew why he was here really. He needed to know more. Miss Walker appeared to be Miss Haversham's closest friend.

Of course, it wouldn't hurt to have some ammunition against the enemy. That was the real reason he was here. Because that's what they were, despite the kiss, and the dog rescue. So long as she pursued this story, he could not let down his guard.

Which certainly meant no more kisses.

No more thinking about her figure either. Or how he'd like to see her hair loose and dry, spilling about her bare shoulders.

Most certainly no thinking of taking her to bed.

No. She was the enemy and he'd do well to remember that.

"I wonder that she has time to walk the dog," he commented vaguely.

"Lower your arm." Miss Walker moved in front of him so that he was speaking to the top of her head. "I wonder that too, sometimes. I think she scarcely sleeps. Between looking after her parents, her writing and helping me, I'm certain she must spend a mere hour or two abed at night."

"She said her parents were ill."

Miss Walker nodded. "Her mother fell sick a few months ago and never really recovered. Her father was forced to retire some years ago due to his eyesight and ill health."

"A blind father as well as a blind dog?"

"Not quite. He just struggles to read, that sort of thing. They had Freya late in life—a surprise baby—so Freya has been looking after them for some years. It's been a struggle, I know that much." She straightened and pressed her lips together. "But I am certain she would not appreciate me telling you so. You must forgive me, Lord Huntingdon. My mouth appears to have run away with me."

"I don't mind, Miss Walker."

Her gaze narrowed, her mouth twitching. "I see."

"You see? You see what?"

"Oh, it's not my place to say," she said breezily. "Though I feel I must warn you, my lord, customer or not, I won't let Freya be hurt."

"Hurt? Why would I hurt her?"

"She's quite a special woman. If it were not for how busy she is, I always felt certain some gentleman would snap her up, but then men can be fools, can they not?"

He made a vague sound of agreement. He couldn't really deny it, given he had kissed her, and followed her, and rescued her dog and given her blankets. None of which added up to how one should really treat an enemy. Unless he ascribed to Kabirdas' philosophy of keeping one's critics close.

Yes, perhaps that was why he should continue to get to know her. After all, if he knew her progress on the story, he could ensure she never found out about The Kidnap Club.

"Miss Haversham has never had any suitors then?"

"She hardly has the time and I suspect the patience. You're the first man she's ever seemed to tolerate."

"Barely tolerate is closer to the truth I think."

"My point still stands, Lord Huntingdon. I will not see her hurt." She waved a pin at him. "She likes to think she's tough, but she cares deeply. About everything." She gestured about the room and Guy had to lean back to avoid a jab from a pin. "Do not let her care about you unless you have good intentions."

He held up a hand. "I have no intention of hurting her."

She eyed him for a few moments then set down the pin and retrieved a needle and thread. "I'm glad to hear it."

"How long has she been writing?"

"Oh as long as I can remember." She licked the end of the thread, held the needle up to the front window and threaded it efficiently. "She started writing serious articles, but the newspapers want nothing to do with her. One of them suggested she try her hand at the gossip, and it went from there. I know she doesn't enjoy it, though."

"I cannot say being on the receiving end of those articles is much fun either."

"Oh yes, I suppose she likely has written about you." Miss Walker shrugged. "I don't read them, and I think my customers appreciate that. I would rather their secrets remain theirs."

"You are one of the few I fear."

She sewed a few quick stitches then had him remove his coat. He handed it over.

"I'll have this ready within two days. Thankfully you only damaged the seams and didn't tear the fabric, or it would be another story." Miss Walker bundled the coat in her arm. "I forgot to mention, Freya wanted to pay for the damage. She came in this morning and said you might pay me a visit."

"Pay?" He blinked a few times. The woman who had holes in her coat wished to pay for the damage to his? "Certainly not."

"I thought you might say that, but she was quite insistent."

"Well, you can tell her there's no chance I am letting her pay."

"Why do you not tell her yourself?"

"I have little idea where she lives," he admitted.

"Princes Street. Number twenty-three."

He eyed Miss Haversham's friend. "Why are you telling me this?"

"I trust you not to hurt her and she needs something pleasant in her life."

Pleasant? He wasn't certain he was capable of pleasant. Distant was usually the accusation. Busy too.

He nodded toward where ribbons were strewn across a table in the rear of the shop. "Which color does Miss Haversham like best?"

Miss Walker turned toward the table, a knowing glint in her eyes. "Blue. Pale blue. It brings out her eyes."

"Gift her that, will you, when you see her? And tell her I don't want any blasted payment."

Her lips twitched. "As you will, my lord."

Dear God, what the devil was he doing?

THE PAPER PARCEL TREMBLED in Freya's hands. She peered at the shiny door knocker, just able to make out her appearance in the metal. She made a face. There was nothing that could be done to improve how she appeared, especially not in a worn, brown coat and her hair tugged into a no-nonsense style under a simple bonnet almost the same shade as her pelisse.

Why did she care anyway? She was not here to impress Lord Huntingdon.

The door eased open slowly and the butler's eyes sparked recognition. "Yes?" he asked in a slight drawl.

"Um, I was hoping to request an audience with Lord Huntingdon."

His gaze flicked up and down her before he backed away and closed the door. She tapped her foot and leaned forward to stare into the door knocker. Good Lord, did she have something in her teeth? She widened her smile and pressed a fingernail between two teeth. The door swung open and she moved her hand swiftly to her side and straightened.

"His Lordship will see you now."

"Oh. Good." She swallowed. She'd rather expected he might decline her or be too busy or something similar. She had also hoped he might, then she had a fine excuse not to see him. And yet she had prayed he wouldn't send her away.

After dispensing of her hat, pelisse and gloves, she followed the butler through the house and ended up at the earl's study once more. The grandeur of the building did not impact her any less than before but she found herself more focused on what would be behind the door. Or more to the point, who. She couldn't cease recalling how he saved Brig, rolling in front of the rider with little care for his own wellbeing. She never thought of herself as one of those sorts who swooned over men or heroic deeds but every time she recalled the moment, she found it a little difficult to breathe.

There was no denying it. This man was no typical earl. She had written about titled gentlemen enough to imagine she understood how they thought and lived. But Lord Huntingdon was a conundrum.

The butler shoved open the door and the earl rose as she entered. She glanced up at him then dropped her gaze, finding it oddly painful to look at him. Stubble covered his jawline and his hair looked as though he'd been pushing his fingers through it. Sort of soft and tousled. Sort of like she might want to feel the texture herself.

She shook away the thought and forced a polite smile.

"Miss Haversham, please take a seat." He nodded behind her and some secret exchange between him and the butler must have occurred as the man left the room, leaving the door slightly ajar. She supposed rich men and their butlers had some sort of covert language known only to rich men and their ilk.

"I won't be staying long," she said swiftly.

The sooner she left this small room, the better. She likened being in his study to being underwater, struggling to breathe. His presence—especially so close—made her chest tight and her heart beat faster. She needed to escape and gulp down some air before she drowned.

"Is something wrong?"

Wrong? She met his gaze. Oh yes. So much was wrong. How could she remain unbiased when she couldn't even function normally in his presence? When she could not forget his kiss or every act of kindness? Her journalistic instincts screamed that he was somehow tied up in the disappearance of these women. The fact that one of those who had been kidnapped was now married to his half-brother was hardly something to forget. Not to mention him evading her questions.

Everything about their acquaintance from start to finish was wrong. She needed to put an end to any semblance of...whatever on earth this was...and go back to being the pesky journalist who would eventually break the biggest story of her life.

"I just wanted to return this." She placed the paper package on his desk and pushed it slightly toward him. "And to tell you that I will pay for your coat."

Scowling, he pulled the string and flipped open the paper. The prettiest ribbon she had ever seen sparkled against the brown packaging. Lucy admitted it was one of the more expensive ribbons, but the earl hadn't asked about the cost, just requested it be added to his account.

So, *so* much of her wished to keep it. To tie it in her hair and loop it around a summer bonnet. To feel pretty and excited that a man gifted her something. To feel anything other than a poor spinster who hardly slept and whose fingers hurt all the time.

But she couldn't. Her journalistic integrity would be brought into question, especially if he really was involved in her story.

"I have no use for ribbons." He pushed the package back across the desk.

"Neither do I." She eased it over once more.

He sighed, picked up the ribbon and moved around the desk, closing the gap between them. "Well, that's not true."

She blinked as he came closer, frozen. Her throat tightened, the pulse in her ears increased in pace. When he reached toward her, her skin prickled. All she had to do was duck away, make an excuse and leave, but her blasted legs would not obey. He reached over, providing her a close-up view of the stubble and his perfectly tied cravat.

"What...?" she managed to whisper, her voice strangled.

"You have so much hair, Miss Haversham. It's quite beautiful."

Some strange noise escaped her. A combination of two words perhaps or maybe more but they just came out as nonsense. Her cheeks warmed and she clamped her lips together. If she could not speak English or even scarper, it was best she remain quiet and try to salvage some sort of dignity.

She felt a tug at her hair then he stepped back. When she reached up, her fingers met the silk tied about her locks. "I really shouldn't..."

"Keep it, Miss Haversham. It suits you far better than it suits me." He rounded his desk and clasped his hands behind his back. "And I will not hear of you paying for the damage to my coat."

"But it was my fault!"

"Did you push me to the ground?"

"Well, no—"

"It was entirely my own fault."

"But what about—"

"Was there anything else?"

"Yes. No. I mean..." She blew out a breath. If she had any sense, she'd tear the ribbon from her head and leave it on his desk. Considering she had rather a reputation for being a woman of sense, her inability to commit such an act was puzzling indeed. So she wagged a finger in his direction. "This does not mean I will cease investigating you."

His lips curved. "I wouldn't expect anything less."

Chapter Twelve

THE CLOYING SCENT OF the woman's perfume almost made Guy's eyes water. He opted for breathing through his mouth as she shrugged her bare shoulders, took his coin and turned away. The baron was known to frequent several whorehouses in London, but he was regretting taking on the task of tracking the man's movements himself. Russell would have been more at ease here or even Nash, but both were married, and he didn't want to put them in that sort of position.

Especially in a less than reputable place like this.

He was no stranger to some of the more elegant places though, even he couldn't bring himself to rid himself of his virginity at the hands of a paid woman. Why Lord Pembroke wished to frequent the less salubrious places, he didn't know. The floors were sticky, the walls were thin and the patrons ranged from drunkards to the criminal sort. Clearly, the man had a specific taste, though Guy couldn't understand it. One would have a damned high chance of coming away with something nasty in a place like this.

Still, he had his information. Lord Pembroke had his favorite here and never failed to visit on a Wednesday. Which meant Lady Pembroke would be alone. At least almost. All he had to do was worry about how they could slip past the men he had guarding her to be able to speak with her. Guy narrowed his lips. The man was known to be a bastard even here. What Lady Pembroke had to be experiencing every day as his wife hardly bore thinking about. The sooner they helped her, the better.

He pushed through the room, easing past the patrons and whores, narrowly avoiding a generous dousing of ale from an inebriated fellow. He stilled before he reached the door, closing his eyes ever so briefly. He had to be imagining it surely? Determined described her to a fault but she'd never be so foolish as to follow him to a damned whorehouse.

Twisting slowly, he shook his head. A man with fists the size of hams, hair sprouting from every inch of him from the back of his neck to the hand he had placed on the wall beside Miss Haversham had blocked her in. It seemed she was more interesting than the whores here, and he had to admit, he didn't much blame the man. Even in that wretched coat, her pale appearance and stubborn chin drew him to her. Now all he wanted to do was knock off her plain hat and see her hair spilling about her shoulders.

Her bare shoulders.

He shoved away the thought. The last thing he needed to be considering was any sort of nudity, especially whilst surrounded by the sounds of beds knocking on walls and various bodies wound around each other with little care for propriety.

Well, she had said she wasn't giving up investigating him, he'd give her that. But, good Lord, did she have to be so bloody insistent on getting into trouble?

She glanced wildly around, a hand to the man's chest as she tried to slip under his arm. He moved, preventing her from stepping about him, then moved again. He shifted closer. Guy pinched the bridge of his nose and pushed between two couples. Miss Haversham's gaze met his and her eyes widened—with relief or annoyance that she had been caught, he wasn't sure.

"Leave the lady be," Guy warned, tapping the man on the shoulder. "She's not interested."

"She'll be interested if I pay enough," he said between gritted teeth, ignoring Guy.

"I told you, I'm not for sale!" Miss Haversham insisted, pushing against the man's chest again with little effect.

"You'll be for sale if I want you to be." He made a grab for her waist and she dodged aside. Then he snatched her wrist, his fingers curling about her with ease, looking as though he could snap her arm in one swift movement.

Guy blew out a heated breath. This was enough. He wanted out of here and he sure as hell wanted Miss Haversham gone. He tapped the man's shoulder again. He turned slightly, just enough for Guy to swing a punch and connect with his nose. Bone crunched and blood spurted from his nose. The man released her wrist and grabbed his nose.

"What the hell—"

Guy ducked a responding blow, latched a hand around Miss Haversham's arm and dragged her from the building. They burst out into the fresh air and Guy whirled on her, releasing his hold. "What the devil are you doing here?"

"Well—"

He held up a hand. "Investigating me, I know, but why would you possibly think it was acceptable to enter a place like this?"

She lifted her chin, her posture going rigid. "*You* entered a place like this."

"No one is going to mistake me for one of the wh—" He paused. "One of the women here, are they?"

"He had to be blind or drunk. I certainly don't look like any of those women."

"You're too damned pretty and fair. Of course a man looking for a certain service is going to find you appealing."

She opened her mouth then closed it.

He blew out a breath. He should not have admitted that. Not just because she knew he found her attractive but because he hadn't wanted to admit it to himself. Now he'd said it aloud, it hung there, like hot sand in the desert, dancing about them. Miss Haversham really did have no intention of backing down and he had little idea what to do with her.

But he also had very, very many ideas of what to do with her. None of which were in any way useful.

ANGER HAD BEEN FREYA'S presiding emotion. First at the man practically holding her prisoner, then at Lord Huntingdon for even visiting such a place. It ruined everything really. Even though she thought she was prepared to follow him in, she hadn't been. Why would the blanket-offering, dog-rescuing, attractive earl frequent such a place? Surely it was only for ne'er-do-wells and those who could afford nothing better.

But then, if she thought too hard about it, she pictured him with some beautiful courtesan who flittered about the richest men of the *ton*. Admittedly, he had never been connected with any of the well-known courtesans but that might have been preferable to him coming to a place like this—a place that reeked of desperation and tragedy.

Oh who was she kidding? It didn't matter where he found his pleasure—the tightness in her chest was only triggered by one emotion.

Jealousy.

She'd laugh if it wasn't so preposterous—acting as though she had some sort of claim over him.

The earl could do as he pleased, and one mere kiss meant nothing. It might have been her first kiss in forever and one that she would never forget but it meant *nothing*. Why was that so difficult to remember?

And now he had inferred he found her pretty. Freya could count on one hand the amount of people who had called her pretty. Most of them included were family members. She had thought herself rather better than such simple flattery, but it seemed not. She sucked down a deep breath. Somehow, she needed to regain her footing here.

"I would not have had to come here if you hadn't, you know," she pointed out, her voice weak. She clenched her teeth together. Just wonderful. What a fine argument that was.

"Of all the foolish things you could do, Miss Haversham, this was the worst." His jaw tensed, covered in thick, dark stubble, highlighted by the lamplight flooding out of the building's windows.

She recalled the feel of it against her mouth, leaving her with the most pleasant warm feeling. "What if I had not spotted you? That man would have taken what he wanted, regardless of payment."

She straightened her shoulders. "I could have escaped," she lied. The man had been three times the size of her and her wrist still ached from where he'd grasped it.

He shook his head. "I thought you a clever woman."

"I am," she protested.

Or at least she was. When she realized quite where the earl was going, she'd been unable to ignore the painful burning sensation inside her. She'd hoped she was wrong. That maybe he was performing some charitable act but then he'd spoken to several of the women and her heart became weighted like a stone.

How silly she had been to believe for one moment he was different from other members of the nobility. They took what they wanted and lived a life of pleasure and debauchery with little care for the predicaments of others. The chances were, he was only being kind to her so she would drop the story.

Well, he wasn't going to continue to fool her.

"I'm clever enough to see that you are precisely who I thought you were," she said more forcefully, taking a step toward him.

"Oh?"

"Nothing more than a pleasure-seeking, reckless rake, who likely finds it amusing to play the hero, knowing he is anything but."

The furrow in his brow deepened. "Pleasure-seeking?" He moved closer. "There's no damned pleasure to be found in there." He gestured to the building.

His gaze searched hers and her heart pounded in response. She regretted the word now. *Pleasure.* It swung between them, like the pendulum of a clock, striking her hard in the chest. There had been pleasure in their kiss, and she was certain more could be had. But that could have been fake. One big lie. A deliberate moment rather than the rash mistake she had thought it to be.

She folded her arms, offering up the only defense she could conjure. "I suppose your favorite woman was not there tonight."

"My favorite woman," he repeated with disgust. "Miss Haversham, I do not frequent whorehouses."

She gestured up and down him. "I rather believe this proves you to be a liar."

"I am here with good reason and not to seek a woman, I can assure you of that."

"I saw you speaking with those women, giving them coin. I saw you and—" Her throat clogged suddenly when she recalled the sharp pain of seeing him with them. She had no claim over him and no desire to have one, she reminded herself.

Not that it seemed to matter.

His eyes narrowed, and he pressed a finger to his lips. "Miss Haversham, are you jealous?"

She gasped. "Certainly not!"

"Why does my private business upset you then?"

"It does not—" She cleared her throat. "It does not upset me," she repeated, lowering her tone. "However, it disappoints me. These places are full of desperate women, doing what they must to get by. As far as I'm concerned, such acts should be done by two people who are both consenting and eager."

"Eager," he murmured, his gaze darkening. "Indeed."

"And as a gentleman, you have to set a standard, and if you cannot be the better man, then who will be?"

He moved closer and her chest tightened. "I'm trying to be the better man."

"Well, good but then why..." She lifted a hand and it connected with his chest. She wasn't certain whether she wished to push him away or curl her fingers into the lapel of his jacket and pull him in. Regardless, he glanced down, the intensity in his expression fading to nothing, and stepped back.

"Go home, Miss Haversham. It's not safe for you here." A crash resounded inside, followed by shouts. She flinched when the door slammed open and several men spilled out onto the ground, a wild tangle of flailing limbs and flying fists.

"Go home," he ordered as one of the men rounded upon him. "I'll explain why I was here tomorrow." He ducked a punch. Barely.

Freya glanced between him and the brawling men. If she remained much longer, she'd end up tangled in the fight too. She had no doubt the earl could defend himself but maybe not with her here. She turned on her heel and scurried toward the main road, the sounds of the fight vanishing into the smoky evening air.

Silly Freya. She should not even want an explanation. He didn't owe her one. But her aching heart wanted it, nonetheless.

Chapter Thirteen

MISS HAVERSHAM'S HOUSE could only be described as modest. Though hardly a pauper's dwelling, the paint around the windows of the tall, skinny brick building was flecked, and when Guy glanced up, he spied a tile about to slide its way from the roof onto some poor unsuspecting pedestrian. The windows and front step were clean, though, so they either kept a maid or Miss Haversham furiously scrubbed them in between work and dog walks. He frowned to himself. He'd wager on the latter. The blasted woman didn't know how to take a rest.

He straightened his cravat and climbed the three steps to the dark blue front door. He didn't really owe her an explanation. Not really. The fact she'd thought he visited the whorehouse for company was laughable considering almost the opposite was true. Nevertheless, he'd seen the truth behind her eyes.

Jealousy had revealed itself.

And he liked it—the fool that he was—he damned well liked it.

Why did he always forget he didn't want a woman? Or more specifically Miss Haversham. He couldn't tell her the truth—not about The Kidnap Club and certainly not about his size predicament that sent every woman screaming from him.

Just one of those things was enough to dissuade him from courting usually. Given there were two secrets at stake now, it gave him a very real reason to avoid her.

Yet here he was.

He rapped the knocker against the door and waited, aware of his pulse pressing furiously against his collar. Guy tugged on it and drew in a breath. Here he was—an earl, a kidnapper, a man of power and means, and his palms were sweating against his gloves.

Pure, utter insanity.

The door eased open and an elderly gentleman peered out at him. His clothes were worn and hanging off his shoulders, as though he had lost weight recently. His eyes blazed with intelligence and curiosity, though, and Guy concluded this had to be Miss Haversham's father.

"Yes?"

"Forgive me, we have not been introduced. Lord Huntingdon, Earl of Henleigh at your service."

Mr. Haversham's eyes widened. "The chap Freya has been investigating." He put a hand to his mouth. "I do not suppose I was meant to say that." He bowed his head. "Mr. Haversham, my lord, what can I do for you?"

Guy let his lips tilt. "I'm well aware of Miss Haversham's interest in me. I was hoping to speak with her."

"Ah. I do hope she's not in any trouble."

"Not at all."

At least not anymore. She nearly had herself taken for a damned whore last night and it still made him grind his teeth to picture that man trying to touch her. Her recklessness was going to be the death of her. Or him. Or both of them at this rate. Which was precisely why he needed to speak with her and put an end to this whole big mess.

"I'm afraid—" Mr. Haversham turned with a frown.

It took Guy a moment to figure out what the noise was. Someone upstairs suffered a coughing fit that could be heard even from Guy's position on the steps. Miss Haversham had told him of her mother's illness, so he assumed it was her.

"Forgive me, my wife is unwell." He pressed a hand to his head. "What was it you wanted again, my lord?"

"I was hoping to speak with Miss Haversham," he repeated.

Another round of coughing echoed down the stairs. Mr. Haversham glanced at the stairs then to Guy. "I'm so sorry, my lord, I think I should go and see to her. My daughter went to purchase some lozenges for the cough. I'm certain she shall be back soon." He backed inside and made his way up the stairs, pausing. "Do feel free to make yourself at home in the parlor room."

Mr. Haversham eased his way upstairs, his boney legs letting loose a crack that made Guy wince. No wonder Miss Haversham had her hands full. Neither of her parents were in the best of health. He motioned for his driver to wait then stepped inside and shut the door behind him and tucked his hat under an arm.

Enclosed in the darkness of the entrance hall, he took tentative steps toward an open door, feeling a little as though he was stepping on hallowed territory. This was where Miss Haversham had grown up. He glanced around for signs of her occupation, spotting a summer bonnet hanging on a hat stand and a simple, childlike embroidery of a thistle on the wall that he imagined had to have been done by her.

The parlor room offered up few hints of her occupation, though. A blanket hung over the back of a worn armchair and various country scenes hung on tired, grey wallpaper. The fire had died to almost nothing, so he strode over and retrieved the poker, stoking it back to life and adding a log. Even once he had the fire going, the chill in the room ate through his winter garments. No wonder her mother remained sick. How could she recover when the whole house had to be close to freezing? Much longer in this cold and Mrs. Haversham would die, especially when winter hit.

It really wasn't any of his business.

In fact, he should leave right now and speak with Miss Haversham another time.

He strode to the window and eyed his waiting carriage then peered down the road for sign of Miss Haversham.

Blowing out a breath, he ran a hand through his hair. Damn it all. How could he leave her mother to die? Miss Haversham would likely hate this idea—hell, she might even fight against it—but if he acted now, before she returned home, he could have her mother safe and warm and hopefully recovering.

He allowed himself a grim smile. Oh, yes, Miss Haversham was going to hate him for this, he was certain of it. But he had no choice.

"PAPA, I HAVE..." FREYA paused on the third step, her hand to the bannister. In her other hand, she clasped the medicine for her mother. "Papa?"

He opened his mouth then closed it and the oddest little smile appeared on his lips. She turned, retreated down the stairs and came to stop in front of him. Her heart beat so hard against her chest she feared it might crack through her ribcage.

"What's wrong, Papa?" This was it, was it not? The moment she had been fearing would come. Her mother was dead, gone without her daughter at her bedside. Though, why her father had such an odd expression she could not say. "Shall I give Mama the medicine?"

He shook his head. "Don't bother, dear. She's not here."

"Oh." A lump formed in her throat. She tried to shove it down and ignore the prickling behind her eyes. This day had been coming for some time now. She should be prepared. And no matter what, she had to be strong for her father. She couldn't lose him too.

"That Lord Hunting chap just whisked her away." He chuckled. "It was all rather amusing really."

"Lord Huntingdon?" She lifted a finger then lowered it, frowning. "Lord Huntingdon was here?"

"Oh yes." Her father nodded vigorously. "Looking for you, though he did not say why. It seems you were not all that secretive about your investigations, Freya. He seemed to know all about it."

"Well, yes..." She shook her head. "That's beside the point. Where on earth did he take Mother and why did you let him?"

"He's a rather commanding chap."

"So Mama has been kidnapped and you just stepped aside and said that was fine?"

He lifted his shoulders. "It hardly seemed worth arguing with him and your mother was quite content to go along after he had a little word with her. He said he couldn't conceivably leave her in such a state and then had his man come in and gather up her belongings and took her off in his coach." Her father's smile expanded. "She seemed to enjoy the whole experience rather."

Freya resisted the desire to slap a hand to her forehead. She left her parents alone for half an hour and look what had happened. Her mother had essentially been kidnapped and her father seemed utterly content about the whole thing.

"He said to be sure to visit whenever I want. He even offered for me to come with him, but it seemed rather an impertinence and I'm quite comfortable here. Besides, I could not very well leave you alone."

"Dear Lord..."

"Freya," he scolded. "Watch your words."

"Sorry, Papa." She exhaled slowly. "You can imagine it is a bit of a shock."

"He seems a fine gentleman and I know your investigations have not turned up anything of note yet. In fact, was he not the one who gave you that blanket?"

"Yes," she admitted quietly.

"Hardly the scoundrel, is he? And what sort of an earl would snatch an old woman up? What nefarious reason could he have?"

"Well, he could...he could be using Mama against me. To dissuade me from my investigations."

Her father eyed her for several moments, his lips twisting. "It sounds to me as though you are rather hoping for continued reasons to investigate him. Were it any other man, you would have likely moved on to other things by now."

She gasped. "Papa, that's simply not true." She tucked the medicine back in her satchel, snatched up her hat and shoved her hands into her gloves. "I'm going to see Mama now. If you do not care what is happening to her, then I must go and fight her corner."

"There is no corner to fight, Freya, your mother is quite well, and the earl will be taking excellent care of her, I have no doubt."

She released a sound of frustration and stomped out of the door, slamming it shut behind her. Damn the earl. Thinking he could just march in and...and take her mother! That was not how things were done. At least not in her circles. She supposed noblemen were quite used to swanning in, snatching up mothers and imagining they knew what was best for everyone. Her mother should be home, in her own bed, under the care of her daughter, not in some strange house with maids she didn't know.

By the time she reached the earl's townhouse—a good hour's walk—her indignation hadn't receded. Indeed, if anything it had pooled into a fiery mass of fury. First he made her watch while he spoke to various ladies of the night and then, when he was likely coming to give her an explanation, he snatched up her mother instead.

Of course, she didn't really have to watch him speaking with those women, but she had hardly been able to avoid it. Nor had she been able to resist the pull at her stomach, the way it still twisted and turned when she imagined him propositioning them. It should not have shocked her, nor had any impact on her whatsoever. She'd seen and heard enough scandal in her journalistic career.

She'd never heard of someone kidnapping someone's mother, though. What on earth had motivated him to do such a thing? Could it be true what she said to her father? Would he try to use it against her? And to think her father considered she was only investigating him because of some interest in him. Ridiculous.

Fine, so she had kissed him and maybe been a teensy-weensy bit jealous of the women, but she was a journalist. A professional. She would not pursue a story she did not think had merit out of some mere fleeting interest in a man.

Lifting her chin, she straightened her back and pulled the doorbell. Professional. Calm. Dignified. She could do this.

Chapter Fourteen

MISS HAVERSHAM'S CHEEKS were mottled red. Guy tried to keep the smile from his face. He'd been waiting for the doorbell to ring.

Well, waiting for her really. He knew she'd hate what he had done. The woman was too darn proud. He pulled open the door fully and gestured for her to enter. "I wondered when I might see you."

"I do not know how you can be smiling when you have essentially kidnapped my mother!" She stepped in and furiously tugged the pins out her hat then thrust it toward Mr. Brown. The man scrabbled to catch it when she released it into his hands. Her gloves followed then her coat, her movements jerky and erratic.

"I did not kidnap her," he said slowly.

"You might as well have done." She put her hands to her hips and stared up at him. "Why did you do it? To persuade me to drop my story? If you think—"

"Funnily enough, I had no motive other than to see your mother well, but I am glad to see you do not think better of me," he drawled.

"Well, why should I?" She peered around, waiting until the butler had slipped out of the hallway. "After all, you were in a whorehouse last night," she hissed.

"As were you, Miss Haversham."

"Yes, well, I was not there for the...entertainment."

"No, you were there to pry into my business, which I must say is getting exceedingly exhausting."

She huffed and turned away from him. "Where is my mother? I demand you return her to me."

He stepped in front of her, his arms folded. She glared up at him.

"Well?"

"She's sleeping. She had some soup and bread and is under the capable care of Ruth, one of the maids, and my housekeeper. I've asked for my physician to take a look at her too. No doubt he will be along shortly."

Miss Haversham stilled and blinked a few times. "She had bread?"

He nodded.

"She hasn't eaten bread in days," she murmured.

"Well, Ruth said she had quite the appetite when they got her settled in bed."

Her posture softened. "And she's sleeping now?"

"As I said."

"I suppose...I suppose I should let her rest. She hasn't been sleeping well with that cough." She tilted her head and eyed him. "Why did you take her?"

"Because she is ailing, Miss Haversham, and in case you had not noticed, I have plenty of room here and enough servants to care for a good deal more people than just me. It seemed rather the logical thing to do."

"You could have at least waited for me."

Guy arched an eyebrow. "If I had waited, you would have fought me every step of the way."

"I might not have done," she mumbled.

He allowed himself a slight smile and she echoed it, her lips curving.

"I might have done, I suppose."

"Let her stay here a while. I have the space and she can stay warm and recover properly here."

Her chin lifted. "I was doing my best."

"I know," he assured her, spying the wounded glint in her eyes. "But you can look after her much better here."

"Me?"

"If you wish to stay with your mother, you are more than welcome."

Her brow furrowed. "You wish me to stay too? Me?"

"Indeed."

"But I have been making your life miserable!"

"Well, it is nice that you could admit that but as far as I can tell, if you are under my roof, I will know exactly where you are at all times and thus my life will be much easier."

"So you did have an ulterior motive?"

"No, but it does seem rather a good plan now, does it not?"

She pressed her lips together and narrowed her gaze at him. "I will stay, but as soon as my mother is well, we'll be going home. I would not wish to be an imposition any longer than necessary. Nor do I intend to fall for any of your trickery."

He lifted a hand. Miss Haversham thought him devious and he supposed she was not wrong. He'd planned enough kidnappings in his life to accept such a description. However, he had scarcely given his plans to help her mother any thought. Mostly, he could not conceive of her suffering through the death of her mother. It pained him more than it should. And, as he said, he had plenty of space.

"There is no trickery here, I vow."

Though, he might very well have tricked himself. Here he was, trying to talk himself out of any kind of desire for the woman and now he had her staying in his house. He wondered sometimes if he was just a glutton for punishment.

Yes, Guy, why not have the woman who cannot know anything about you under your roof where you can see her every day? Why not offer yourself the chance to imagine her in the room a few doors down from yours, slipping naked into the sheets? Why not—

Good God but he was a fool.

"You know you still owe me an explanation for yesterday."

"Ah." He'd rather thought she might have forgotten that. "Over dinner."

"But—"

"Take the carriage home. Inform your father what is happening and gather your things. Bring him along too if you like." At least if her father was here, he'd be a lot less tempted.

"I'm not certain he will come..."

"Then we can discuss this over dinner."

"I—" She lifted a finger then dropped it. "I suppose that will do."

It was a small victory but a victory nonetheless. He still hadn't quite figured out what he was to tell her, but he hoped he could be vague enough not to give away any details. Miss Haversham might be a determined woman who wrote bloody awful gossip columns but there was no chance she was the callous, gossip-gathering person he thought her to be. If he appealed to her caring side, she might just understand.

As she left and he shut the door, he met Brown's gaze. "Don't say a bloody word," he told the butler.

He shook his head. A victory. To have her here. Under his roof. What an idiot he was to believe that.

"FREYA?"

Freya jerked awake from her position beside her mother's bed, her elbow slipping from where it had been resting on the arm of a chair. She jumped up before she had fully remembered where she was and put a hand to the wooden pillar of the bed to steady herself.

"Yes, Mama?"

She smothered a yawn and perched herself on the edge of the bed. Her mother peered at her from beneath a mountain of blankets and surrounded by plush pillows. Without a doubt, her mother was far more comfortable here than at home. The sumptuous damask silks and golden tassels alone had to be worth more than their entire furniture collection.

She didn't know if Lord Huntingdon had been responsible for choosing the room in which her mother stayed but it was decidedly feminine, with little touches of pale green combined with muted gold and cream. Furnishings from the far east sat alongside older English pieces, combining to make a most elegant room. If she let herself, she could be quite envious of such a room, though she had already been assigned a guest bedroom and it was hardly squalid.

"I did not know you were here." Her mother attempted to push up from the bed.

Freya jumped up and aided her with sitting. Maybe it was wishful thinking, but she swore her mother looked better already. This recent illness had taken its toll, her face growing gaunt and the dark circles around her eyes more prominent.

They shared similar pale hair but her mother's had grown thin and wispy with the white in it appearing more stark. Their facial features were similar too. At least they had been until her mother had sickened. But color shone on her cheeks for the first time in weeks.

"Lord Huntingdon has been kind enough to let me stay whilst you are here," she explained.

"He seems a good man. Quite commanding. I like that in a man." She paused, a cough wracking her.

Freya patted her back and waited for the fit to subside before offering her a drink. Her mother took a few sips and handed it back. After setting it on the table, Freya moved back to the chair on which she'd been sleeping. She scarcely recalled falling asleep which indicated quite how tired she must have been. Her neck ached from the silly position and it felt as though she had bruised her elbow from being perched on the hard wood.

"How are you feeling, Mama?"

"Better for having some sleep," she said. "And I ate a fair amount earlier." She smoothed her hands over the bedding. "What a lovely room this is." She looked to Freya. "Is your father well?"

"Quite well. He is staying at home with Brig. I think he will enjoy the peace and quiet without us womenfolk."

Her mother smiled. "No doubt. I know my ill health has been worrying him."

"Mama—"

"This Lord Huntingdon—he must be quite interested in you to wish to look after your mother."

"Oh no, not at—"

"Men like that do not do such acts without motive."

"Well, actually, I think he's rather in the habit of doing such acts," she admitted quietly.

"A good man then. And rich too." Her mother waved a finger at her. "Do not be too stubborn to give him a chance."

Freya shook her head, feeling a few spirals of hair bobbing loose from her impromptu nap. "I doubt a man like him would be interested in me. I'm sure if he wanted someone, he could have his choice of women." She straightened. "Besides, I am quite comfortable with my status as spinster. Why should I wish to give that up?"

There were more reasons too, but she certainly was not going to tell her mother that her hallowed rescuer frequented the worst whorehouses in London.

"Because there is no weakness in loving another. It takes strength to depend on your husband and, so long as he depends on you too, you shall be most happy, of that I have no doubt."

"Mama, I am not here for a husband."

"You need someone to look after you," her mother insisted. "You take too much on those small shoulders of yours."

"I'm perfectly fine on my own. I have lasted this long after all."

"Freya—"

The dinner gong echoed through the house and Freya's stomach gave a little tumble. She had chosen her best dress, but it was hardly suitable for an evening dinner in a fine house. The pale muslin had recovered from its dip in the puddles, but its long sleeves were a little crisp and the bodice slightly too tight. She tugged at the itchy lace at her wrists and eased out a breath. She looked smart at least. Hopefully that would make up for her lack of ornamentation.

"Try to at least be a little charming, my love," her mother ordered. "And fix your hair!" she added as Freya scurried out of the room.

She shoved the strands of hair back into clips as she made her way downstairs and turned left then paused and turned right. Lord Huntingdon waved from the open doorway of the dining room and she hurried toward him. "Am I late?"

"To a dinner for two, hardly."

"Oh good." She huffed out a breath and dropped her hands from her hair. A traitorous strand dropped immediately down her shoulder. She grimaced when his gaze landed on the long length of it, sloping its way down her bodice.

"May I?"

She nodded and stilled, her spine as straight as a ship's mast. He took the long length of her hair and she felt the tug and pull of a pin. "I didn't know earls were versed in women's hair," she said lightly in a bid to hide the tremulous quality of her voice.

"Oh earls are versed in just about everything," he said, coming around in front of her and offering a slightly lopsided smile. "You have about the most amount of hair I've ever seen. I do not know how women do it."

She touched the back of her hair. "It's my one concession to vanity I suppose."

"It is quite beautiful." His throat bobbed. "Shall we?"

He offered her an arm and led her into the dining room. She nearly paused on the threshold and considered escaping when she spotted the golden candelabras, the shining chandelier above and the long, gleaming oak table, laid with enough food to feed a sizable family. What on earth did she think she was doing here?

Chapter Fifteen

GUY COULD NOT QUITE fathom when Miss Haversham had become beautiful. Though even that word felt a disservice.

Stunning.

No.

Spectacular.

Not that either. It was something else, something no man could put his finger upon. When he first met her, he'd considered her a little plain. Then he had conceded there were interesting things about her. The pale skin for example and the inquisitive eyes.

Discovering the full length of hair that skimmed down to her hips when she had shoved him into the pond had done something odd to him. He kept picturing her bare shoulders with it spread over her milky skin. Touching a lock of it made that image worse because now he found himself imagining it draped across *his* skin.

She sat to his right, her eyes as wide as the dinner plates as she eyed the food spread across the table.

"Is all well?"

"Um." She gestured to the food. "I hope this is not in aid of me."

He waved a hand. "Not at all. Any extra will be given to those in need."

She shook her head. "I should not be surprised that you dine like this every night."

"It's just how it's done."

"Do you never question why?"

He peered at her. "Why?"

"Why this is how life as an earl is done? Do you never question your duty to the title?"

He lifted a shoulder. "In some ways, I suppose." He could not claim kidnapping troubled women was exactly part of his duties.

He aided her in loading her plate with food. A footman filled her wine glass then brought around quail roasted in a fragrant, tangy sauce. Her stomach grumbled in response and she grimaced. Guy pressed his lips together and glanced away from her. She really did look uncommonly pretty, especially without adornment in her hair or any jewelry distracting from the bare expanse of her décolletage. There was something to be said for ridding oneself of all the fuss required for such dinners usually.

"What of you?" he asked.

"Me? I do not have any noble obligations in case you had not noticed."

"I was speaking of duty. Do you never question yours?"

She blinked a few times. "What duty?"

"To your ageing parents. Your friends." He lifted his brows. "Your dog...?"

"Why would I?"

"It would be nice, would it not, to take a little time for yourself occasionally?"

"Time is the privilege of the rich," she said blithely.

"Oh yes, time," he drawled. "I have so much of that."

"Well, you must be an exception."

"If I had a wife, no doubt she would have endless time on her hands, but I cannot say the same for most landed gentlemen. It occupies most of one's time simply running an estate, let alone several."

"I see." Her throat bobbed and she took a quick sip of wine. "Is that why you visited the—" she glanced around "—place of ill repute. So you could, um, relax?"

Allowing himself a slight smile, he shook his head. He wondered how long it would take her, and by his approximation, it was all of twenty minutes. "I went there for business of a sort."

"I'm certain many women who work there think of it as...business." Warm, rosy splotches of color appeared on her cheeks and she stabbed her quail with a fork several times.

"I went there to help someone."

Her gaze shot to his. "One of the women there?"

"Someone else."

"But who?"

He eased out a breath. He should have known a mere snippet of information would not be enough for her. "If I were to tell you that a woman needed my help or else she could end up in grave danger, would that be enough for you?"

Her gaze searched his, a little furrow appearing between her brows. "Perhaps. What sort of danger and what kind of help could be found at a place like that?"

"I needed to know the movements of a certain person. One who visits that place."

"So you could then help this woman?"

He nodded.

"I see." She eyed her plate for a few moments then lifted her gaze to his. "I suppose that makes sense."

"That's it?"

"That's what?"

Guy chuckled. "No more questions?"

"Well, I have many, but I can see you do not wish to tell me more, and if what you say is true, I doubt this woman wishes a stranger to know her business."

"It is true, and you are right. The fewer people who know her troubles, the better."

Though, like a fool, a nagging part of him wanted to reveal all. He really must be addled. How could he forget this woman was in pursuit of a story that could ruin him, and everyone involved?

"I'm really not certain why you did not tell me this yesterday," she murmured.

"Would you have believed me? Especially when you were looking very much like you wanted to see me strung up for being there?"

Miss Haversham straightened in her seat. "I do not think I looked like that at all, and I would have been fair."

"Doubtful."

"I would have," she protested.

"I think you were quite jealous of me speaking with those women."

As soon as he said the words, he wished he could conjure them back. Yes, he believed that to be true but why the devil did he think to say it aloud?

Whatever this unspoken thing between them was, it did not need bloody well addressing. It needed burying, somewhere deep. Maybe the center of the Earth, though he suspected even that wasn't deep enough.

This vow to avoid women forever, was getting mightily old and tiring, though.

Not to mention rather impossible at present. It seemed no matter what he did, Miss Haversham ended up in his life. Or possibly he kept engineering it that way. He needed to see his doctor perhaps. Have his sanity checked.

Several moments passed of Miss Haversham staring at him with her mouth ajar. Finally, she lifted her shoulders. "I certainly wasn't jealous. You may do whatever you wish with your spare time, my lord. It has nothing to do with me."

She jabbed a fork aggressively into what was left of the quail and Guy forced away a smile. Jealous, to be certain. But he really, really should not like that fact one jot.

Not one damned jot.

"MR. BROWN, I DO NOT suppose you've seen Lord Huntingdon, have you?"

The butler peered at Freya from underneath patchy white eyebrows. He always looked somewhat amused at her presence and she could not tell if he liked having her here or thought her beneath him but, as yet, he had been kind to her mother and her.

"I do believe he is in the stables, miss."

"Thank you." She twisted then twisted again, eyeing up each of the doors.

Brown's lips quirked and he pointed to a door at the rear of the hallway. "Through there, miss, then follow the corridor into the rear drawing room."

"Right. Thank you."

Her shoes tapped on the shiny tiles as she made her way through the house until she reached soft, luxurious carpeting. She had not even known of the existence of this room and she could not help feeling like an intruder in the pristine, powder-blue room.

A piano occupied one corner by the long windows that let in streams of sunlight and a small circle of delicate chairs occupied the center of the room. She couldn't picture Lord Huntingdon sitting on any of the chairs, so she imagined this room was hardly used.

It served to remind her of their differences, something she kept forgetting. Though her own home had two drawing rooms, they only used the one in the colder months. It never looked this clean or untouched either, and the furnishings were worn, old and patched together in places.

See? No matter how similar they seemed in their ethics, their worlds could not be further apart.

A breeze wrapped itself about her when she stepped outside, pressing her skirts to her legs. She shut the glass-paned door behind her, clasped her hat in place and scurried in the direction of the stables. It took a moment for her eyes to adjust to the darkness of the interior after the bright daylight of the courtyard.

TAKING THE SPINSTER

Horses shifted in their stalls at her presence, but she saw no sign of the earl. A strange scraping sound snared her attention and she marched down the stalls in the direction of the noise.

Her breath came to a standstill in her lungs. She couldn't be certain what she expected to find but it wasn't this.

Shirt sleeves rolled to just above his elbows, no cravat and afternoon stubble shading his chin, Lord Huntingdon carved away at a strip of wood, sending flecks of it flying about him. The muscles in his arms flexed, making her mouth a little dry. If the scraps of wood on the floor were anything to go by, he'd been doing this for some time.

"Lord Huntingdon?" she managed to rasp.

He stilled, dropped the wood on the table in front of him and straightened, shoving a hand through his disheveled hair. Sawdust clung to the dark waves and she longed to brush them loose, so she clamped her hands at her sides.

"Miss Haversham. What can I do for you?"

"I was wondering when—" She leaned to peer past him. "Is that a perambulator?"

His lips curved marginally. "Of sorts. It is not quite finished yet."

She rounded the table and smoothed a hand across the wood frame. "It's beautiful," she breathed. "Who is it for? Is your new sister expecting a child?"

He shook his head, that vague amusement still on his lips.

"I don't mean to criticize but it's a little smaller than most I've seen. Is there a reason for that?"

"It is lighter than most perambulators. Intended to be able to be pushed more easily. I also designed with a certain, ungrowing occupant in mind."

Freya glanced up at him. "Ungrowing? I do not understand."

"It's for you."

"For me?" She pressed a hand to her stomach. "But I am not pregnant!"

"No." He smiled. "For The Brigadier."

She eyed him for a few moments her lips parted. "For Brig?"

He nodded and folded his arms, drawing her attention to the firm muscles of his bare forearms. "So you no longer have to carry him to the park."

She sucked in a sharp breath, her chest almost painful. He had made this for her. To save her from carrying her dog. God Lord, this man was too much.

"You really should not have..." Her throat closed over and she tried to swallow the tightness several times and failed.

He shrugged. "I like making things and it seemed a worthwhile project."

Her vision clouded over, her eyes stinging. She turned away and sniffed.

"If you hate it..." He put a hand to her arm.

"No, it's not that," she whispered. "It's just..." Tears dripped down her cheeks, one plopping unceremoniously on the straw beneath her feet. "It's just no one has ever done anything as nice as this for me before."

"You deserve it," he murmured.

Lord Huntingdon twisted her toward him and brushed away a tear with a thumb, his finger pad leaving a little hot trail on her skin. She met his gaze and swallowed hard. Sunlight from the narrow window of the stables highlighted his strong jaw and the intensity in his gaze. Every inch of her froze, knowing what was to come.

And there was no chance she would deny him. How could she? He had carved this with his bare hands just for her. Or for her dog. Either way, it was the singular most kind thing anyone had ever done.

He closed the gap, putting a deliberate hand to the base of her spine to inch her in toward him. He gave her all the time in the world to deny him, to push him away or utter a word.

Freya lifted her chin and closed her eyes. His lips met hers slowly, gently as though savoring some sort of delicacy. She issued a tiny moan at the feel of him against her and she splayed her hands over his chest, able to explore the carved muscles beneath the thin layers of fabric. He tasted her with his tongue, lazily exploring her and giving her all the time in the world to relish his kiss. Her heart thudded erratically, and her skin heated from top to toe.

Hands sliding down to his arms, she gripped him in an attempt to draw closer and kiss deeper, but he stilled abruptly. His hand dropped from her spine and cold air assailed her. She opened her eyes slowly and glanced at him from beneath heavy lids, aware of the warm, puffy state of her lips. His shoulders shuddered slightly, and he stepped back even farther, issuing a regretful sound from the back of his throat.

She flattened a hand to her pounding chest. "I—"

He huffed out a breath. "What was it you wanted anyway?" he asked sharply.

"Oh." She'd practically forgotten why she had sought him out. "Oh, yes, um I was wondering when the physician would be coming?"

His furrowed brow intensified. "Is your mother worse?"

"No, quite the opposite," she said hastily. "I was just hoping to let her know when we might expect him."

"At around three I believe. I received a missive from him this morning."

"Good. Excellent." She clasped her hands together in front of her. "Well, I suppose I should..." She loosened her hands and jerked a thumb toward the exit.

"Yes, you should."

So much of her longed to stay. To ask why he had ended the kiss, to beg to know why he had not taken it further. She hardly had a wealth of experience with men, but she had received a few kisses in her lifetime and had even been coaxed into bed with one man several years ago. She knew how eager menfolk were to take a willing woman to bed. So why had he backed down?

She dropped her shoulders and hurried to the courtyard, pausing outside and letting the cold wind chill her heated skin. He had backed down because he did not really want her. That was the only explanation. Maybe he felt sorry for her or perhaps even liked her—as an odd sort of a friend. Why else would he help her mother and her silly old dog?

But women like her did not end up in the beds of earls, and she should not want it either. She had seen how poor women were treated by rich men time and again—cast aside, often pregnant and forgotten. If she was clever, she would do everything she could to keep away from such a fate.

What a shame her usually clever mind did not seem to want to work around him. She would have to try much, much harder not to fall for him.

Chapter Sixteen

GUY PACED TO THE WINDOW, paused and peered out at the dark streets then paced back to the fireplace to warm his hands over the flickering flames. The sun had set a good hour ago and dinner would be in another hour. Miss Haversham knew that. So why had she not returned home?

Home? He stared sightlessly at the painting above the mantelpiece. This was not her home, and with how her mother's health was improving, she would be leaving soon. A heavy weight settled in his stomach at the thought and he shoved away from the carved marble fireplace with a huff. He had no claim to her, no reason to be concerned over where she was. He wasn't her father, her husband or even her lover.

By God did he want to be, though.

He gritted his teeth, paced back to the window and squinted into the night. Lamps glowed at intervals along the road, highlighting the occasional pedestrian and setting his heart racing then dropping when he realized it wasn't her.

He couldn't deny it. He wanted her. Every inch of her. Just the recollection of kissing her made him hurt. But the trouble was, he wouldn't be the one to be hurt if they continued. Well, perhaps his ego would be, but no woman could manage him, of that he was certain. Amelia hadn't been the only encounter like that, though hers had been the worst because he had been convinced she loved him and would be willing to try. If his bloody fiancée didn't want him to bed her, no other woman would, and he wasn't willing to hurt Miss Haversham for the world.

The door inched open and he jolted around. "Brown," he said, unable to keep the disappointment from his voice.

"I take it Miss Haversham is not yet home."

"She has not returned to my house yet, no," he corrected.

Brown's lips flickered then moved into a sharp, straight line. "She will be home for dinner I am certain, my lord. The girl hardly seems the disordered sort."

"It hardly matters. She can go hungry if she really wishes."

"Of course, my lord." The butler's lips did that odd little quirk again.

Guy sighed and stared down the butler. "What do you want, Brown?"

"Oh, nothing at all, my lord. Just wanted to see if Miss Haversham was with you."

"Well, as you can see, she is not," he said irritably. "Now cease your prying and go do whatever it is butlers do."

"We only run the entire house, my lord. Nothing much."

"I shall tell Mrs. Bellamy you said that," Guy warned him. "See if she agrees."

"If you wish, my lord." He ducked his head and backed out of the room.

Clenching his jaw, Guy turned his attention to the window once more. Damn the man. He found it entirely amusing for some reason that he had taken in Miss Haversham and her mother. Was he such a bastard that he would usually ignore such pleas for help? He would have done it for anyone, naturally.

Brown had little idea of his involvement in The Kidnap Club, but the man knew him well. Guy did not think such an act should have surprised him.

Movement caught his eye and he moved swiftly back from the window, settled into the armchair by the fire and retrieved the book he had left splayed on the table. He squinted at the text, but the dull candle and lamplight made it near impossible to read. That, and the fact he found himself listening for the front door. It thudded shut and muffled conversation between Miss Haversham and Brown resonated through the walls. Finally, soft footsteps made their way toward his door.

He froze, book in hand, aware of his every breath. The footsteps stilled. But the door did not open. He eyed the door. Blast, was she—

The door opened and he turned back to the book, forcing a concentrated expression.

"I am sorry it's so late." He saw her walk toward him from the corner of his eye.

"Hmm?" He lowered the book and glanced at her. "What did you say?"

"I was just, um, apologizing for returning so late."

He waved a hand, moved the bookmark to the open page and placed it on the arm of the chair. "I'm not your keeper. You may come and go as you please."

"I am your guest, though."

She moved closer to the fire, holding her still gloved hands to it. A tremor ran through her and he grimaced. He should not ask. It was nothing to do with him. Besides, the chances were she was chasing down gossip or trying to find some evidence of his involvement in the disappearance of those women. He couldn't forget she was essentially the enemy here.

"Where were you?" he asked, the question rushing out before his brain could stop him.

"Lucy had been offered some food from one of the large houses she makes garments for, so we spent most of the evening distributing it."

He lifted both of his brows. "Ah."

"I had only intended to help her with an important commission, but I could hardly say no, could I?"

"No, I imagine not." And now he felt a real ass for getting annoyed at her for not returning home sooner.

Not her home. Why could he never recall that?

"Is my mother well?"

"She is in excellent spirits."

Miss Haversham smiled. "She has improved so quickly. I am not certain I will ever be able to repay you."

"You could give up on this idea that I need investigating."

Her smile broadened. "Never."

"So you still believe I am some awful, evil man responsible for the disappearance of all these women?"

She scanned his gaze. "I think you have a secret or two, yes."

"And the evil part?"

"I have yet to decide on that."

He rolled his eyes. "Of course."

"If it's any comfort, I'm not any closer to figuring out your secrets."

"Good."

"Ah, so you do have at least one." Another tremble rippled through her.

Guy rose. "I didn't say that." He glanced her over, closed the gap between them and put his hands to her shoulders to direct her into the chair.

FREYA SWALLOWED HARD.

"You're frozen."

"I am fine," she lied through gritted teeth in an effort to prevent them from chattering. Being some sort of damsel in distress to him was getting a little tiring.

Even if she did like it when he took charge.

No one ever took charge in her life before and she had to admit, there was something nice about it.

But she could not let herself give in. She already revealed herself to be a fool, offering herself up for one kiss then two. He made it clear he did not want her, so she needed to keep herself on guard every hour of the day. If only she were not so bone-tired and cold. It would make being strong a lot easier.

"Do as you are told for once," Lord Huntingdon ordered.

She allowed herself to sink into the chair, aware of how her feet throbbed in her shoes. The plush cushions settled around her, and if it were not for this ridiculously handsome man in the same room, she could close her eyes and fall asleep with ease. But his furrowed brow and the strong slashes that counted for brows kept her fixated on him.

She'd never been more confused in her life and she did not do *confused*. Investigating was about looking at the evidence in front of one and coming to a firm conclusion. The trouble with Lord Huntingdon was she could come to no conclusion at all. Did he like her, did he not? Was he involved in something nefarious or was he simply a ludicrously heroic man?

He kneeled in front of her and she frowned. "What are you—"

Taking one hand in his, he pushed the buttons of her gloves through the holes, one by one. Such a simple act yet she found herself captivated by the strong, sure fingers making light work of the fiddly buttons. Then he drew the glove off slowly, set it over the arm of the chair and reached for the other one. He repeated the movement, adding her second glove to the chair.

Finally, he clasped one hand between both of his and she sighed at the warm touch of his slightly calloused hands—hands worn by the work he had been doing on the perambulator, she assumed. She was not privy to many lords' hands, but she would wager few felt like this, like the hands of a man who actually worked hard. They made her feel less embarrassed by her own scratched, sore and rough hands.

He rubbed his palms over her hers, warming them. "Your hands are like ice," he murmured.

She nodded, her mouth dry. He massaged her fingers then moved on to her other hand. He kept his gaze lowered, concentrating on warming her hands until they were pink, and all sensation had returned. She watched him, eyeing the dark waves of his hair that glinted with hints of gold in the lamplight and the firm slopes of his face. Her gaze fell to his mouth and she recalled how his lips had felt on hers, how swept away she had been.

This act felt no different. Here he was, taking charge of her welfare, allowing her to stop and cease thinking for a mere moment. It didn't matter if she was cold because he would fix that, it did not matter that she was tired because he had a solution for that too. She would be fed, warm and rested by the morning.

It was hard to not like it. Hard not to like *him*. For so long, she had depended only on herself. As her mother had said, depending on another could also be a sign of strength.

Except, he did not want her in that way, and this was temporary.

She snatched her hand back and his gaze shot up. "I'm warm enough now, thank you."

He rose to standing and placed hands behind his back. "Of course." He dipped his head slightly. "I'll see you at dinner then."

Freya nodded, avoiding his gaze. She had offended him, but it was the only way. She could not let herself sink any deeper into whatever this was.

She stared into the dancing flames of the fire until he left and waited a few moments more to be certain he had gone. Then she made her way upstairs and eased open the door to her mother's room. Seated upright in bed, an empty bowl sat at her bedside, and she clasped some embroidery in her hands.

"Oh, I have not seen you sew a single stitch in forever," Freya gasped.

Her mother twisted the sample toward her, revealing a mess of stitches, and made a face. "I'm very much out of practice."

"But it is a miracle." She shut the door behind her and paused at her mother's bedside.

Her mother scowled. "Whatever is the matter?"

Freya shouldn't say. She couldn't.

She flung herself down on the bed, her forehead landing on the soft mattress, her arms splayed beside her. "It's a disaster," she said against the blankets.

"What is, my love?" Her mother smoothed a hand over the back of her hair.

Freya twisted to view her, her cheek pressed against the soft fabric. "I like him, Mama. I really like him."

Her mother gave a knowing nod. "I know you do, dear. I know."

Chapter Seventeen

GUY JOLTED AWAKE, GLOOMY darkness greeting his narrowed gaze. He listened for a moment, but his heart thudded too hard for him to hear anything. Rolling, he peered up at the wooden canopy above his bed until he could make out faint squares.

Damn it, now he was wide awake for no reason and he can't have fallen asleep many hours ago.

He stilled. There it was again. A decidedly feminine cry. He bolted from his bed, sheets tangling around his bare legs. "Bloody…damn…stupid…thing…" He disentangled himself with an aggressive rip then shoved his legs into the breeches he'd discarded over the back of a chair the previous evening.

Barreling out of the door and into the hallway, he realized he hadn't lit a candle and the hallway, with its lack of windows, was darker than his room. Still, he didn't slow his pace and paid for it when he slammed his toe into a console table he should have known was close by.

"Bugger."

One would think years of traversing this short hallway would be enough for one to know where a blasted table was.

"Lord Huntingdon?"

He spun to find Miss Haversham emerging from her mother's room, a candle in one hand. Her loose hair curved around her nightgown, landing nearly to her hips, and her eyes were lidded and sleepy. He swallowed hard and gestured toward her door. "I thought...that is..." He frowned. "Did you hear a cry?"

She nodded. "My mother. A small nightmare but nothing terrible. She has settled now."

"I see." He drew in a lengthy breath. Why did his heart insist on pounding still? The suspected danger was gone.

Well, he supposed if one considered a fair-haired, sleepy woman dangerous, that would explain his racing heart that had seemed to jam itself up into his throat.

She lifted the candle a little and her eyes widened. He let his scowl deepen then noted the way her gaze travelled the length of him. His feet were cold on the wooden floors and he recalled his bare shoulders and torso. In his haste, he'd failed to throw on a shirt and he rather loathed sleeping fully clothed. A silly thing to do considering he had company.

Her lips parted.

Hell fire, there was the danger. In her wide eyes and sweet, slightly open mouth. It stirred his insides, making every inch of him tight and hot. Including his damned cock. If he wasn't careful, he'd make a fool of himself. A *big* fool of himself. And she would run for the hills.

He forced himself to look beyond the pale outline of her figure toward the shadowy painting to the right of her. Great-great Aunt Edith. Hardly an attractive woman. Not to mention his aunt. Her long nose, practically invisible chin and beady eyes were a combination that not even the most talented painter could make look attractive.

"Lord Henleigh, is all well?" She moved to the right a little, directly into his line of sight.

He sucked in a breath through his teeth. No ugly aunts would solve this situation. He needed to turn around immediately and return to bed. A simple task really. One that could be achieved with but a few mere footsteps. If he just twisted a little...

Guy stepped forward.

No, damn it, that was not how it was done.

Her gaze fell upon his chest again, and now he had closed the gap a little, he saw her chest rise and fall quite rapidly.

Very well, if he could not turn away himself, he could at least tell her to return to bed. That would be easy. Just utter the words.

"Bed."

He winced. Now he sounded as though he was demanding to take her to bed. And now *images* assailed him. Her hair brushing her naked body. Then brushing his. The delicate breasts he could just make out beneath the fragile fabric of her nightgown filling his palm. The indent of her waist and his hands curved around it.

He would be hard pressed to make this any worse.

"That is, you should return to bed," he managed to croak out.

She lowered the candle onto the console table and the glow caressed one side of her, affording him a fine view of the shape of her waist against the basic cotton chemise. He'd seen women in garments more tantalizing and complex, covered in ribbons and lace with low-cut necklines. Of course, none of them had let him touch them after they realized quite what he had to offer them, but none could compare to Miss Haversham in this dull length of fabric. It allowed him to peruse her without distraction.

Jaw clenched, he waited for her to do as she was told.

More fool him. When had Miss Haversham ever done what she was told? She moved toward him, almost like a ghost, her footsteps scarcely making a sound on the floorboards. Palm outstretched, she ceased moving when her hand connected with his chest. He hissed out a breath, aware a tremor ran through him. God damn, he was so sex starved that a mere palm had the most ridiculous effect on him.

Or perhaps it was more to do with the owner of the palm. He certainly could not recall this kind of reaction to Amelia's touches. He let his frown deepen when she added her other palm and splayed her fingers.

It would be quite easy to snatch her wrists and ease her away from him. Tell her to be a good girl and send her on her way. It would certainly save him from the risk of her noticing how stupidly well-endowed he was.

Apparently, he liked doing things the hard way.

Correction, the very hard way.

FREYA SUPPOSED PLENTY of women wanted to touch the earl's chest. That was why he didn't react as though she needed to be bundled up and chucked into the nearest asylum. He allowed her exploration of the hard planes of his chest as though this was a common occurrence.

She did not much like the thought of other women touching him, but she did not blame them. Especially whilst the candlelight gilded his muscles, drawing attention to the dips that lined his stomach and the line of dark hair that went from his bellybutton down into his breeches.

Sucking in a harsh gasp of air that felt more heated than it should, she jerked her head up and away from what she had just seen. It had to be a trick of the light, but it appeared there was a significant bulge in his breeches.

Her body pulsed at the idea, leaving her hot and wanting to tug open the buttons of her nightgown. It might as well have been the height of summer in this dark, gloomy and cold hallway or perhaps someone had lit a fire beneath her feet, because every part of her enflamed at the idea he might, just might, be feeling aroused at her simple touch.

His chest rose and fell rapidly, matching the quickening of her own breaths. She marveled at the sheer strength of him. It was quite one thing to feel the hardness of his body beneath his clothing but an entirely different matter to have it spread out in front of her, apparently for the taking. She suspected she could while away many an hour merely touching him.

Something she should most certainly not be doing. But it seemed her hands had a mind of their own.

She traced down past his pectorals, further and further until—

He snatched her wrists. She met his gaze and he held her firm. Her mouth dried as his gaze searched hers. Somewhere in the distance, a carriage rattled by and an owl hooted. Hours might have passed, or it could have been seconds, she wasn't certain.

Then he moved suddenly. She waited to be cast aside, steeling herself against the disappointment.

His mouth came upon hers in a sudden rush. He released her wrists and shoved a forceful hand under her hair, gripping the back of her neck. His other hand snatched her waist and she released a brief squeak of surprise that he quickly swallowed with his kiss.

He gave her no quarter and she did not desire it. Everywhere there was hardness. His body flattened against hers and his mouth urged hers open with no delicacy. His tongue swept forcefully into her mouth. Freya met his kiss with similar intensity, unable to respond in any other way. Her stomach twirled and tensed, her mind raced but landed upon no other firm conclusion apart from needing more.

More kisses, more touch.

She stumbled back a few paces, her back meeting wall. He used the opportunity to take everything she had to give, kissing her over and over until she had little idea where she ended, and he began. The hand on her waist moved up to cup a breast and she moaned against his mouth while he palmed it roughly. He continued his exploration of her, moving over her waist while stealing her breath with his every kiss. He curved his hand down to her hip, and she flexed into the touch, the ache at the core of her building. If he could kiss her like this...

Just imagine what he could do to your body.

"Freya," he murmured, breaking away oh so briefly. The sound of her name on his tongue had her practically collapsing in a mess of desire.

"Please," she begged, shifting her hand down between them.

He grabbed her wrist and moved it away, then snatched the fabric of her shift. He hauled it up and cool air touched her heated thighs. She tilted her head back and rested it against the wall while he kissed his way up and down the arch of her neck, nibbling her earlobe and lips and back down again, sending shivers of pleasure through her.

He continued to draw up the fabric until she felt herself revealed to him. His fingers slid over. Slowly. Far too slowly. She lifted her hips toward him in invitation. Every inch of her pulsed in expectation.

The earl met her gaze as she eased a leg up and over his hip and she gasped at the first touch, widening her eyes. Desire flared in his eyes. He touched her wet heat and pulses of pleasure rocketed through her. Then he slipped his finger between her folds.

Her breaths came hard and fast in anticipation. He groaned when he sank a finger in her and kissed her ardently, swallowing a tiny whimper from her. He moved in and out of her, flicking a thumb over her most sensitive spot then added a second digit, moving faster. The pace grew frantic and she writhed against his touch, drawing out each fragment of pleasure while he kissed her face, her lips, her body, even drawing her nipples into his mouth through the fabric of her chemise.

Pleasure caught up to her suddenly. It overtook her unexpectedly and she dug her nails into his arms, leaning her head back for support. Eyes clenched shut, she rode out the last waves until it left her warm and faintly pulsing. When she eventually opened her eyes, she found him staring at her intensely. He inched his hand away and she rather expected him to abandon her, but he helped her roll down her shift then pressed a kiss to her forehead.

"Go to bed," he murmured, his voice gritty. "Be a good girl for once in your life."

Freya nodded numbly and hastened back to her room. She shut the door and pressed a hand to her racing heart. What on earth had they just done?

Chapter Eighteen

"YOU LOOK A LITTLE TIRED, Guy, are you sleeping well?" Rosie asked as Russell aided her with her coat and hat.

Tired. Ha! Tired didn't even describe it. He was caught in that strange agitated version of tired when one hadn't slept a wink and felt groggy yet entirely too stimulated by life.

Stimulated? What a terrible choice of words. It was bad enough he failed to forget the feel of Freya beneath his fingertips, or the sound of her reaching her peak without adding words like *stimulated* into the mix.

Russell eyed him. "You are not wrong, Rosie. You haven't even shaved this morning, Guy."

He put a hand to his jaw automatically and grimaced at the roughness there. How had his valet let him leave his bedroom like this? Though, truth be told, Long could have told him he had a forest sprouting from his chin and he wouldn't have paid him any notice.

How could he when a few hours before he had been touching Freya, kissing Freya, damn near taking her to bed? He hissed out a breath. What a fool he was, so damned close to revealing himself. If she had not been wrapped up in the pleasure, she would have noticed the size of him surely? And then she'd want nothing to do with him.

"Did you forget we were visiting today?" Rosie asked, putting a hand to her hair to ensure the dark curls were still perfectly coiffed.

"Not at all," he said quickly. "I've been busy, that is all."

"I was hoping to address this problem we are having with Lady P—" Russell clamped his mouth shut and peered around Guy, a brow raised.

Guy swiveled and found Freya standing at the rear of the hallway, her hands twined together. She shifted from one foot to the other.

He tried not to think on the figure he'd felt underneath the simple pale gray gown.

Tried and failed.

"Miss Haversham, what a delight!" Rosie hastened over to her. "Whatever are you doing here?"

She glanced to the floor. "Well, um..." Her gaze moved to Guy's, her expression helpless. "Lord Huntingdon?"

"Miss Haversham and her mother are staying with me for a while." He tried to keep his expression as neutral as possible, especially when he felt Rosie eyeing him closely.

"Oh, I see." Rosie tilted her head. "Well, no wonder Guy forgot we were visiting with him today. He has a household full."

"Hardly," he said dryly. "And I did not forget."

"Yes, you did." Rosie grinned. "But we shall not blame you, I promise."

"My mother is unwell," Freya explained hastily. "We would not be here unless it was absolutely necessary."

"Absolutely necessary," Russell repeated with a twist of his lips. "So I take it her mother could not be nursed in Miss Haversham's home?" he murmured to Guy.

"No, she could not," he replied through his teeth.

Damn it. He'd thought briefly having his brother and Rosie here might be a welcome diversion from the distraction that was Miss Haversham, but it seemed not. Neither Rosie nor Russell were fools and likely saw straight through all his excuses.

"I shall go attend to my mother," Freya said, dropping into a brief curtsey. "Do excuse me."

"Oh no." Rosie stepped in front of Freya. "You must join us for tea."

Goddamn it. Freya met Rosie's gaze and Russell gave Guy a nudge with his elbow.

"I wonder who will win," he whispered. "My bet is Rosie. She's the most persuasive person I know."

"And Miss Haversham is the most stubborn," Guy replied.

"I really should be..." Miss Haversham thrust a thumb toward the stairs. "My mother needs me."

"I need your company more," Rosie insisted. "We can talk whilst they speak on whatever boring brotherly thing they enjoy conversing about."

Guy ground his teeth together. Usually, it contented Rosie to join in with whatever conversations they had. The woman wasn't one for idle gossip or silly chit chat. If she was, she would have never married Russell.

Whatever game she played here, Guy did not like it. He had a sneaking suspicion his new sister had designs on them being together, which was utterly preposterous but there was no way to explain to Rosie that firstly, Miss Haversham was an independent woman who did not much care for the nobility, and secondly, he could not have a woman anyway. The latter part would be the hardest part to explain. He'd rather not have to reveal to his brother's wife the true nature of his...issue.

Not to mention, how the hell did one have anything with a woman that one could not tell the truth to?

"I do believe Mrs. Haversham is sleeping, miss," Brown piped up from his position by the front door. "She asked not to be disturbed."

Wonderful. Was the whole world against them?

Freya narrowed her gaze briefly at Brown and Guy swore he heard her sigh. "Looks like I am able to join you then."

"Wonderful." Rosie clapped her hands together.

"Told you Rosie would win," Russell said with a grin.

"Miss Haversham is at a disadvantage with the three of you against her," Guy muttered. "It's hardly a fair win."

"I'd wager when she goes up against you, she wins every time."

If one counted being kissed and touched until she cried out in pleasure winning then she had certainly bested him last night.

Guy shook his head and motioned to Brown. "We'll be taking tea in the second drawing room." He motioned to the four of them. "For all of us."

Brown's expression grew smug and Guy glared at him. Did he really have to suffer his brother and sister attempting to matchmake as well as the help? Much more of this and he was going to leap up on the coffee table and announce to everyone he had an appendage of abnormal size and no bloody woman wanted him so could they leave it at that?

With Freya in the same room as him he would be lucky if he did not end up sent to the asylum by the end of the day. Somehow, he needed to keep his wits about him.

FREYA LIKED ROSIE. It frustrated her as she did not want to. She'd already concluded the woman was pleasant after their meeting at the coffeehouse, but she really, really liked her now. It made wanting nothing from Lord Huntingdon all the harder.

It also made this whole kidnap story more difficult to follow. If the earl was involved in anything untoward, it would impact his brother's wife to be certain.

If only Rosie behaved like other women of the *ton*. It would make this situation much easier.

Of course, Freya's story was beginning to wither like a neglected houseplant. With her mother staying here and the distraction that was the earl, she had failed to follow up anymore leads or gain more information from him.

Leads? She nearly snorted to herself. Her one lead had been Lord Huntingdon, and she had let him touch her in a most intimate manner. No wonder her investigation was grinding to a stop.

Freya glanced at the grandfather clock in the corner of the room and set down her cup. She should cease pretending these people were her friends. They had been her living for quite some time and would continue to be if she could not complete her story of the missing women. If she ever wanted to move away from writing that blasted awful column, she needed to gain some perspective.

"Oh you are not leaving us, are you?" Rosie said.

"I really must check on my mother," Freya lied.

Well, half-lied. She hadn't seen her since this morning and did like to check on her at least twice a day. However, her health had recovered so well of late, she suspected her mother did not need her, especially with how well the earl's servants had looked after her.

"If Miss Haversham wishes to go, you cannot keep her captive, Rosie," Guy said tightly.

"I'm hardly keeping her captive, Guy." Rosie made a face at Lord Huntingdon. "I'm simply enjoying her company."

"I've enjoyed yours too," Freya admitted.

Apart from Lucy, she didn't really have any female friends. Or friends at all rather. Her relationship with Lucy worked because they both knew what it was like to be so busy that one scarcely had time to sit. If she let herself, she suspected she could view Rosie as a friend. The woman exuded warmth and intelligence and had some rather unique stories, not to mention her family adored dogs, so they had plenty to talk on despite their different circumstances.

"I hope I shall be able to meet her once she is better." Rosie smiled. "Do give her my best."

"I will, thank you." Freya eased out of the room after her goodbyes and hastened up the stairs. The sooner she escaped, the better. These people were not her friends, the earl was not...well, anything. Simply because he had touched her and made her feel things she had never dreamed of feeling did not make any difference to the situation.

She had a story to pursue, and if she did not, her situation would never change. Her earnings would remain paltry, she would have to continue to have to write about who was bedding whom and her parents would continue to suffer for lack of money.

She paused at the top of the stairs and drew in a long breath then straightened her shoulders. She had not come this far to be swayed by a few kisses and some rather intimate and delicious touches. Yes, she liked Lord Huntingdon, and yes, he had to be about the most handsome man she had ever met. Unfortunately, she could no longer deny that. However, simply because he had a lovely sister and interesting brother, did not mean they were going to embrace her as something, well, more.

Because there could never be more. She rubbed her forehead. She had no intention of becoming a mistress—the sort of woman Freya often wrote about—and clearly Lord Huntingdon had no desire for that either. If he did, he would not have sent her to bed. These little slips of concentration could not happen anymore. She was resolved to putting an end to it.

All she had to do was think of the story. *Not* of Lord Huntingdon, *not* of his kind family, *not* of how wonderful he seemed...

The story! She shook her head. That was where she needed to remain focused. Perhaps she needed to visit the spot where Rosie had nearly been taken. That could help give her some clues as to the identity of the kidnapper perhaps.

There, see? It was not that hard.

Freya inched open the door to the guest bedroom and found her mother sitting by the window, embroidery in hand. She twisted to view Freya when she entered. "I saw that lovely lady arrive. Have you been taking tea with her?"

"So you were not asleep." Freya lifted a brow.

"No, who said that?"

She waved a hand and joined her mother by the window. "It does not matter."

She drew up a chair and peered out at the busy street. Carts and carriages rolled by, people meandered along the pavements and those with jobs to do moved with swift efficiency. Two distinct sets of people. Those like the earl and those like her. Lord Huntingdon would never understand the struggles of her life nor would his family. These people were not her friends.

More importantly, Lord Huntingdon would never be her lover.

She gulped down a breath when she felt heat enter her cheeks.

"Are you well?" her mother asked. "You look a little warm."

"I'm quite well, Mama. But what about you?"

"My chest is tight still, but the cough has almost gone. Mrs. Bellamy brought me up the most delicious broth earlier and it does wonders to loosen it." She shook her head. "I do not know how we shall repay Lord Huntingdon for his kindness."

Freya pressed her lips together. "Neither do I."

Her mother continued with the embroidery but gave her a sideways look. "That little matter you confessed to me...has anything changed there?"

She shrugged.

"I know I can trust you not to be ridiculous, Freya. You are the most level-headed woman I know. However, I do not think the earl is the sort to take advantage of a woman."

"He is not." Freya knew that first-hand. He could have taken advantage of her last night, but he sent her away.

"Perhaps he truly cares for you."

"I believe it is simply in his nature, Mama. We are nothing special." She paused. "*I* am nothing special."

"Well, that's not true, my dear. You are the most wonderful person I know, and if Lord Huntingdon does not see that he is a fool."

Freya did not bother to protest. The trouble was, he was the cleverest of them both. He recognized that despite this attraction, it would never work between them. Now she just had to convince herself of that.

Chapter Nineteen

GUY ROLLED OVER. HE groaned. "Brown? What the devil is it?"

He could not deny he'd rather hoped the person shaking him awake was Miss Haversham. To see Brown's creased features, its rolls and crags highlighted by candlelight, was a lot less pleasant than coming upon Miss Haversham's features.

Brown straightened. "Lady Clearbury, the Duchess of Newhampton, is here to see you, my lord."

He shoved up from his bed. "Now? Here?" He squinted in the direction of the clock on the mantelpiece but could not make it out. "What time is it?"

"Just gone four in the morning, my lord."

"Bloody hell." He rubbed a hand across his face and shoved back the sheets. "Did she say what she wanted?"

The butler shook his head. "She is in a state, my lord. I tried to put her in the drawing room, but she said she would wait in the hallway for you."

Grimacing, Guy rose and swiftly donned a shirt. Brown aided him with shoving his arms into a robe and he tied it tightly at the waist. Whatever Lady Clearbury wanted, it could not be good if it warranted her visiting him in the middle of the night.

"Go back to bed, Brown," he told the butler. "There's no sense in us both being awake, and I suspect the duchess is not here for tea and cake."

Brown nodded, paused at the doorway of the bedroom and gave him an odd look.

"What is it, Brown?" Guy snapped.

"If she is to stay..." He glanced at the floor. "Well, if I may be honest, my lord, Miss Haversham might feel a little...put out?"

"Damn it, Brown, the duchess isn't a lover." He glared at the butler. "When have I ever brought a woman home?"

"Until Miss Haversham, never, my lord."

Guy gritted his teeth. Yes, he was very aware of the fact he'd never let random women stay in his home. Family members or dinner party guests, that was it. Though the butler might not be aware of his virginial status, he knew Guy was not in the habit of cavorting with women, which made Miss Haversham's stay here a source of great interest for the staff, no doubt.

"Brown, go to bed," Guy repeated wearily.

"Of course, my lord."

Lighting a candle once Brown had retreated, Guy made his way downstairs to find the duchess pacing the hallway as promised. Brown had lit a single lamp on the hallway console table but even he could see the tear tracks and red eyes. She hastened over, still wearing her pelisse, hat and gloves.

"Oh, Henleigh." She flung her arms around him, burying her head against his chest.

He eased the candle down onto the nearest table and put a hand to the back of her head then carefully eased another around her trembling body. She smelled of smoke and the tiniest hint of perfume, telling him she had been entertaining or partying prior to this visit.

She sobbed against him and he murmured what he hoped were comforting words. Crying women were not his specialty, as Miss Haversham had proven. Her tears had been more than he could stomach and kissing them away had seemed the most logical thing to do. He had little desire to kiss the duchess, even if it had made Miss Haversham stop crying, however.

Finally, the sobbing slowed, and she lifted her head, easing away from his hold. "I know I was not meant to come here but I did not know where else to turn." She tugged a handkerchief out of her sleeve and dabbed under her eyes. "I could not very well tell my husband and you said I must keep quiet about my sister." Her chin trembled and she shoved the handkerchief back into her sleeve then pulled a letter out of the other.

Guy took it from her and unfolded the scrap. "He will kill me," he murmured. The words were scrawled in what looked to be charcoal, written at an odd angle in almost incomprehensible writing. "This is from her?"

She nodded, pressing fingers to her lips. "A newspaper boy delivered to me only an hour ago. He said she had slipped him the note when travelling in her carriage."

"I see."

"She would have been with *him*," she said, her mouth pinched. "I fear there is no time. What if he harms her before we can save her?"

"I will not let that happen. I have a man watching her. We will ensure her safety. If we need to intervene, we will, I promise."

Lady Clearbury nodded slowly. "Every day that she is with that monster brings her closer to death."

"I know." He put a hand to her arm. "We have been trying to find a way to bring her out safely, and without notice, but should the time come that we need to act, it will be done, I vow."

"Oh thank you, Henleigh. That reassures me greatly." She flung her arms around his neck and squeezed him for a moment before releasing him. "I shall leave with haste before anyone notices I am here. Please, please send me word should you make any progress."

"Of course," he promised.

He ushered her out, shutting the door gently behind her and blowing out a breath. He had not wanted to act any sooner than was necessary, but if Lady Pembroke deemed it necessary to get word to her sister, the situation must be dire indeed. He turned away from the door and stilled before he could grab the candle.

"Miss Haversham, what exactly—"

She took a few steps toward him, her jaw tense and her posture stiff. "I was right," she muttered, thrusting a sharp finger in his direction. "You *are* having an affair with the duchess."

"AN AFFAIR?" HE REPEATED.

Freya nodded, pressing her tongue against the roof of her mouth. Her chest hurt. The image of him embracing the duchess lingered in her mind and she suspected it would not vanish for some time. How foolish she had been to believe he was anything different from the rest of Society.

"Freya, she—"

"It's Miss Haversham to you," she said archly, shaking her head. "To think that you would conduct an affair whilst my mother is ill under your roof. To think that I—" Her voice cracked. She drew in a breath. "To think that you touched me so just yesterday," she hissed. "You must think it all quite amusing."

"Believe me, there's nothing amusing about this." Lord Huntingdon's lips pulled into a thin line. "I was not conducting an affair and there was nothing amusing about touching you. Damn it, Freya, that was the most—"

"I do not even want to think on it."

She twisted on her heel before the lump in her throat could turn into something else. Her cheeks were hot, splashed with indignity. How amusing it all must have been to see her swoon over his every act, all the while he likely planned to use her and discard her as so many men of his ilk did with women of reduced circumstances.

"Well, I want to think on it." He moved swiftly around her, blocking her escape up the steps. "Believe me, I cannot forget it."

She glanced up at him briefly and, for a second, she believed him. The intense furrow in his brow, the darkness of his gaze, the tenseness in his jaw. It all led her to believe he might very well have truly wanted her.

"You are a fine actor," she murmured and went to step around him.

He moved to block her path again. "None of this is an act. Or was an act. Or..." He released a breath. "There was good reason the duchess visited me, and we are most decidedly not having an affair, I promise you."

"Then why the furtive meetings with her? Why the embrace? You cannot tell me these are the acts of an innocent man."

"They are not."

She felt herself deflate. Well, this was what she had wanted, was it not? For him to confess the truth. But some silly little part of her had wanted a better reason—one that meant he truly cared for her and all this kindness had meant something.

"Well, at least you can admit that much. Now if you will please step aside, I will gather our belongings and we can leave you to your—" she waved a hand "—liaisons."

"You're not going anywhere, and your mother still needs to rest."

"I thank you for your kindness to her, of course," she said formally. "But I think it is time we remove ourselves from this ridiculous situation." She shook her head. "To think that I—"

"To think that you what?"

"Nothing at all." She forced a smile. "You shall get your wish, my lord. I shall leave you in peace finally."

"Perhaps I do not want you to leave me in damned peace."

She scowled at him. "Why ever not?"

"Because..." He issued a frustrated breath, shoved a hand through his hair and wrapped a hand around her wrist. "Come and sit. I cannot do this here."

"Do what?" Her heart gave a little jolt of anticipation. She let him lead her through to the dining room and set her on a chair then watched while he lit the two lamps on the table. She stared up at him as he paced past her, pivoted and stopped a little distance away.

"What is going on?" she demanded. "I really think I—" Freya tried to rise but he motioned for her to sit so she remained.

"You are right about me not being an innocent man. I am wholly guilty of many criminal acts."

She frowned. This was not quite where she had anticipated this going. "Criminal acts?"

His jaw tensed. "You recall I mentioned a woman needing help when I went to the whorehouse?"

She nodded. "The duchess was the woman?"

"Not quite." He shook his head. "Lady Clearbury came to me tonight because she received word from her sister—a woman who is trapped in an abusive marriage and is allowed to see no one, not even her own sister. Her sister, Lady Pembroke, fears she will be killed by her husband."

Freya opened her mouth but could not fathom how to respond. She detected no hint of a lie but was this all part of his act? Was he continuing to pretend to be the benevolent hero so she would fall into his arms? Though, if he had truly wanted her in his bed, if she was honest, he could have had her the previous night. Yet he sent her away.

"You were right about those missing women. I am involved."

She should have felt triumph but instead her chest thudded with a hollow ache. "How are you involved? And why?"

"They come to me, needing help. I work with four other men and women. We take the women under the guise of a kidnap, ensure they are protected and aid them with a new life if such a thing is needed."

She blinked a few times. Of all the conclusions she had come to about his involvement, she could not have fathomed this. "You kidnap them? You, The Earl of Henleigh, kidnap women?"

He nodded, drew out a chair and angled it so he could sit in front of her. "My father was not a kind man and I know what it is like to live with such a beast."

"He hurt you?"

"On occasion," he admitted, "but he had to stop as soon as I grew taller than him. My mother took the brunt of his behavior."

"So you wished to help other women in such a situation. But why kidnap them?"

"My cousin was trapped in such a marriage. You know there is no way for a woman to divorce her husband and the law finds it entirely acceptable for a husband to discipline his wife."

"Yes," she muttered. "The law is not kind to battered women."

"I asked two friends of mine to aid me in spiriting her away in such a way that she would not be chased down or be blamed should she be discovered."

"No one can blame a woman for being kidnapped," she murmured. "And I suppose they would assume she was dead when she was not returned for ransom."

"Precisely."

"But how does the duchess know of this? And the other kidnaps? You were involved in your new sister's kidnap, were you not? She was not married at the time."

His lips quirked. "That was a little accident. And word is spread extremely quietly."

"There were the other kidnappings. The ones where the women came back."

"Occasionally a woman needs to disappear just for a while. One of our other members needed to escape an arranged marriage until she was of age. So we helped her vanish until it was safe."

Freya shook her head in wonder for a while. It was more than she could have imagined and, sweet Mary, what a story it would make. A group of nobles kidnapping women to aid them in their escape.

"If this ever gets out, Freya, those women will be in danger."

She nodded slowly and sighed. "The story of a lifetime and I cannot tell it..."

"You understand why."

"Of course." She met his gaze. "I will not tell it, I swear. But you must promise to answer all my questions. I have many."

He smirked. "I would not expect anything less, however, you might wish to ask all of us your questions."

"All of you?"

"The Kidnap Club." He gave a dry chuckle. "It seems they think you would be a worthy member."

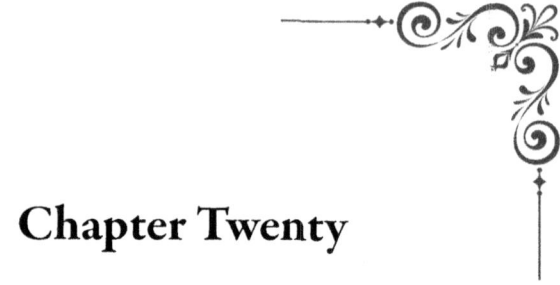

Chapter Twenty

FREYA TAPPED HER INDEX fingers together repeatedly. Guy moved the reins into one hand and leaned over and folded his hand over hers. "There's no need to be nervous."

"Oh, I'm not nervous." She kept her head turned slightly away from him, her gaze fixed on the passing countryside.

He allowed himself a knowing smile. Freya might be one of the boldest women he'd ever met but he knew when she was nervous.

Her shoulders lifted as she took in a deep breath then she turned toward him. "Tell me, what happens if they decide I should not be taking part in all of this?"

"Well, we shall have to kill you of course."

She blinked at him several times then a brow rose. "You are teasing me."

"Naturally." He offered a quick smile. "Rosamunde is already determined you are to be our newest member. Her husband would never argue with her and Nash is usually content to go along with whatever decisions are made. Grace will most likely make up her mind about you after you meet. She's the analytical sort."

"I recall writing of their nuptials, but I confess, I do not know much about Lady Southam."

"We kidnapped Grace."

"Oh my."

Guy nodded. "It is how they met. She needed to hide away for a while. I cannot say I approved of their relationship initially, but Grace has been a steadying influence on Nash."

"And I imagine you are happy that your friend has found love," she said, nudging him with an arm.

"Oh, yes, that too."

She rolled her eyes. "Such a romantic."

The woman had no idea. No idea at all. At this point, he'd concluded they had little choice but to bring her in. He didn't like it for a few reasons. Firstly, the group had expanded a little too much. The fewer people involved, the better. However, Grace and Rosamunde were more than useful members. Grace with her rather large intellect was able to find solutions to almost any problem and Rosamunde was about the boldest of them all. Having a woman with connections did not hurt them either.

Still, he'd have preferred to keep Freya out of it. For most of them, should anything be discovered, their ranks might protect them. For Freya, he could not be so certain and there was only so much he could do. The thought of anything happening to her because of him made his chest tight.

"We're here," he announced, drawing the buggy to a halt outside of a dilapidated farm building. Set amongst the gentle slopes of the Surrey countryside, the grey stone building offered little more than shelter from prying eyes. Tiles were missing from the roof and the door hung off its hinges. Guy stepped down from the carriage and assisted Freya in climbing down. She paused, straightened her skirts and eyed the building.

"This is your meeting place?"

"For now. We change meeting place regularly these days. It's safest that way."

"Goodness."

"Goodness?"

"When I started following you, I could not have fathomed this was what you were up to."

"No. I was some evil abductor of women, was I not?"

She gave him a look. "I only thought that briefly."

"I knew it." He gestured inside, noting the horses tucked around the rear of the building. "Come, it looks as though the others are here."

He pushed open the creaky door and he ushered Freya in. Daylight seeped through the holes in the roof and the shutterless windows whilst everyone gathered in the center of the building. Nash gestured to the roof. "I want it noted this is my least favorite place to meet."

His wife, a dark-haired woman of extremely small stature, shook her head. "This is the best, Nash. I already counted the number of people we saw on the road and there's a far less chance of being spotted here than any of our other meeting places."

"Must you be so logical," he grumbled.

She blinked a few times. "Always."

Freya glanced around at the four other people, her posture stiff. For some reason, Guy's chest tightened for her. Why, he did not know. It seemed important that the other members accept Freya but then he supposed it was, after all, if they took her into the group, she would never write about them.

Not that he ever expected Freya would now. She was many things—determined, stubborn, far too hardworking—but she cared far too deeply to put the women they helped at risk.

"I'm so glad you are here," Rosie said with a smile. "I just knew you would be perfect for us."

"Thank you." Freya clasped her hands together. "I'm glad to be here."

"Russell tells me Miss Haversham here has made quite the impression on you, Guy." Nash offered a sly smile. "She must be special indeed for you to want to bring her in."

Guy glared at Nash and his grin widened.

"Actually, Lord Huntingdon told me of your latest problem," Freya said before he could come to her defense.

Of course, the woman did not need him running to her aid. She was so used to doing everything alone. He could not help but wish she'd let him help her a little more, though, at times. Or a lot more.

Not that such thoughts were helpful right now. He'd already come too damned close to giving in and sweeping her into her bedroom and to hell with whatever she thought of him. But he couldn't. He'd scare her. Maybe hurt her. He just couldn't do that to her.

"I think I could help," she continued. "Naturally you are all known to Pembroke, but I will not be. No one knows my face."

"Oh yes." Rosamunde nodded. "Your anonymity could be quite useful."

"I thought I might pretend I am looking for work. I could get into the house to speak with the housekeeper then try to make contact with Lady Pembroke."

Guy glanced around. Russell shrugged. Grace frowned for a few moments, drew out a notepad then nodded.

"It's a better solution than any we have come up with." Nash pointed to Russell. "Since it became known he's your brother, it's been harder for Russell to go unnoticed, and Rosie already attempted to call on her but had no luck."

"It's settled then. I shall go enter their house and speak with Lady Pembroke."

"Not without me you will not," Guy said tightly.

Grace shook her head. "But everyone knows you, Guy. It makes no sense for you to accompany a maid."

"I'm not leaving Freya alone in the house of a known bastard like Pembroke."

"Guy..." Russell warned.

He lifted a hand. "I shall remain hidden, but I refuse to send her into danger alone."

Freya twisted toward him. "I'm sure I can manage—"

"Don't argue with me on this," he told her. "For once in your life."

She eyed him for a few moments before sighing. "Very well. I shall go into the house and you can remain nearby. Happy?"

Guy grimaced and Nash caught his eye, his smile far too smug for Guy's liking. When had he gone from being entirely in charge of this club to essentially being told what to do by all the female members?

"HOW IS YOUR MOTHER?" Lucy asked, glancing up from her sewing.

Freya paused too, flexing her aching hand. "Much better. I think I shall have to bring her home soon."

"Have to?"

"Well, I can hardly trespass on the earl's hospitality for much longer. It would not be right."

And if she stayed, she could not guarantee she would ever want to leave. The man had put his reputation, his life on the line to help women for years now. The more she learned about him, the harder it was to avoid the truth of the matter. He might have privilege and wealth, but he was no average member of the *ton*. Unfortunately, that made her like him all the more.

It made her like him too much.

If this continued, she might well end up falling entirely, head over boots in love with him, and where would that leave her? Penniless reporters did not marry earls. Not to mention he kept pushing her away. She would be a fool to stay longer than necessary.

Lucy lowered the fabric and needle to the table and rose, moving around where they worked to retrieve a biscuit from the nearby plate. She handed one to Freya and took a large bite of her own. Freya set down her work and nibbled on the edge of it while Lucy leaned against the back of a chair and eyed Freya.

"I think the earl will not want you to leave."

Freya shook her head. "He will, trust me."

"I saw how he looked at you when you were here before."

"Yes, with annoyance."

"And he bought you the ribbon, and he took your mother in when she was ailing."

"And he made Brig a perambulator," Freya added then paused, putting a hand to her mouth.

"He did what?"

"He made Brig a perambulator so I would not have to carry him to the park," Freya admitted.

Lucy yanked out the chair next to Freya, dropped herself down on it and shoved the remaining biscuit in her mouth. "Wait a moment. He *made* it? By hand?"

Freya nodded grimly. "It is quite beautiful."

"Dear God, he must be in love with you."

A laugh escaped her. "Love? That's preposterous."

"Why else would an earl of all people make your dog something *by hand* if he did not love you?"

Freya lifted a shoulder. "He is just that sort of person. He sees a problem and wants to fix it."

"Not unlike someone else I know." Lucy eyed her. "And this also explains why you are dropping the story you thought would make your career."

Freya eased out a breath. Not telling Lucy everything was the hardest thing in the world. "I am dropping it because there is no story."

"You were so certain for so long, Freya. There must be something there, though I cannot believe it is anything nefarious. The man helps sick mothers and old dogs, it seems. Hardly the sort to prey on poor little society women."

"He isn't," she confirmed. "And so I have nothing to write about."

"Or there's still something but you are too in love with him to reveal it." Lucy pursed her lips. "Though, what could it be if he's too good a man to harm anyone?"

The story of a lifetime, Freya admitted silently. If she wrote about an earl kidnapping women to escape beastly members of the nobility, she would never want for work again. Every paper would want her to write for them. But she couldn't do it. Not to Lord Huntingdon and not to the women he'd aided.

"Lord Huntingdon would not harm anyone," she confirmed. "And there is no story."

"So what will you do now?"

Freya discarded the half-eaten biscuit on the table, her appetite gone. Not because Lucy had hit on anything, of course. Loving an earl would be ridiculous for a woman like her. It happened too often. They ended up tossed away like her biscuit, used up and often pregnant.

Lord Huntingdon would never do such a thing, of course. She knew that because, honestly, he could have taken her willingly to bed last week, and he did not. Instead, he'd left her with the oddest, sweetest kiss on the forehead and sent her away.

It did not take her investigative skills for her to realize nothing would ever come of whatever was between them. No love, no silly ideas of marriage, no stolen moments together. Lord Huntingdon did kind things because that was who he was. He was entirely incapable of being anything else.

She was nothing special to him.

"I will have to find another story I suppose."

"I'm sure one will come up. What of that man you were investigating recently? The baron?"

Freya hadn't explained why she had decided to delve into his business dealings to Lucy, but she had concluded if she was going into enemy territory, any information she had on him would help.

"He is not a good man, I know that much."

"Well, then that's your story. He might not be an earl, but if he is involved in something nefarious, you have a duty to write about it."

Freya nodded slowly. "You're right." So now she just had to find the time, in between aiding The Kidnap Club, and the rest of her duties, she would need to dig deeper into the man's past.

"I still cannot believe the earl made you a perambulator." Lucy shook her head with a smile. "If I were you, I would have fallen at his feet and begged him to take me then and there."

"Lucy!"

She chuckled. "You are a better woman than I."

Freya wasn't so sure. If the earl had wanted her, she would have given herself. She probably still would. She had a horrible suspicion that even one night with the earl might be worth the heartbreak that would follow.

Not that her heart could be broken anyway. One had to be in love with a person for that to happen, and she certainly was not in love with Lord Huntingdon. Not at all.

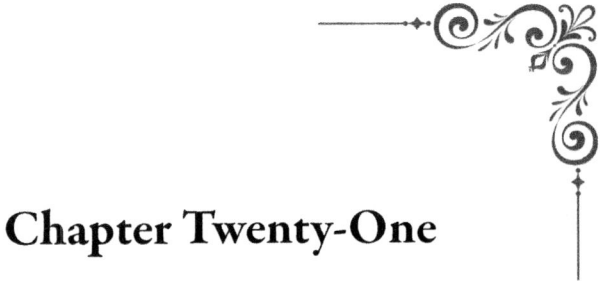

Chapter Twenty-One

"I'VE CHANGED MY MIND."

Freya fixed Guy with a look. "You cannot just change your mind."

He peered around her at the townhouse. No sign of the skulking henchmen could be seen, but from what Russell had said, they were always present, watching over Lord Pembroke's wife. "I can and I have. You're no longer part of The Kidnap Club."

"I will be fine." She put a hand to his arm, drawing his attention to her. "No one shall pay any attention to me."

"They shall if you get to Lady Pembroke."

"Believe me, I am quite well versed in not being noticed."

"*I* noticed you, if you recall."

Her cheeks reddened a little. "Well, yes, that was just because you are the suspicious sort."

It was more likely that one could not miss Freya. Or at least he could not. Her pale skin and fair hair, and stupidly innocent eyes and pointed chin, and tiny waist were all far too noticeable. Someone was going to spot her, and she would get into trouble and his hands were tied. How the devil would he protect her once she was inside the enemy's house?

"I don't like it. We'll come back another day."

"I have already arranged an interview as a maid. I'm going inside," she said firmly.

He rubbed a hand over his jaw. Had anyone ever been able to tell Freya to do anything? He doubted it. But he was sorely tempted to throw her over his shoulder and lock her away somewhere until she gave up on the idea of stepping foot in that house.

"If there is any sign of danger, you leave, understand?"

She nodded. "I'm no fool. All will be well, I promise." She hesitated, rose slightly on her toes then backed away, giving his arm a little, awkward tap. "I will be back soon. Stay out of sight."

He gave a grunt. Since when had he been the one taking orders? From his position across the street, the trees hid him from view, but he had full sight of the house. His gut tightened when she went around the back and vanished from his view.

What a terrible idea. The worst. Even Russell kidnapping the wrong woman could not be as bad as this. He should never have offered her a role in the club or even listened to the others. Hell, who was in charge anyway? Him or them? It would have been easy to keep her quiet. Freya might be ambitious, but the bloody woman hauled a blind dog everywhere. Hardly the sort to turn in a group of people trying to help vulnerable women.

Of course, now he'd forced her to give up the story that would make her career. That niggled him too. He was half-tempted to go out and create some sort of scandal just so she'd have something to write about. He just could not quite figure out what would match up to that of an earl kidnapping society women.

A carriage pulled up outside the house and he held his breath. Lord Pembroke had returned—and he was damned early. According to Russell, the man spent every Wednesday afternoon drinking in White's. They'd anticipated he would be gone for at least another four hours. The man stepped out of the carriage and headed straight up the stairs and into the house.

Guy clenched his fists. Freya would still be being interviewed surely? She couldn't be anywhere near his wife. Not yet.

But what if she was? And what would any man who was keeping his wife under watch do as soon as he returned home?

He'd go to her of course. And then he'd come upon Freya. And then God knew what might happen. It was no good. Hiding in a damned tree would not help Freya. He had to get to her.

He didn't need to figure out a plan. One had already implanted in his mind when they'd arrived. The tree at the side of the house would give him access to one of the windows on the second floor and was out of sight. Climbing the mature tree would not be much of a problem—he just hoped the windows were easy to open.

Then he could slip inside, find Freya and drag her out of there.

And hopefully not get caught.

Waiting until the streets were quiet, he hastened across, making a show of looking at his pocket watch when someone passed by with a tip of his hat. Once the man had gone, Guy slipped around the side of the house, flung off his hat and jacket then hauled his way up the tree, his boots scraping against the bark. Brown would have his head for the state of his clothing after this.

He peered into the window but saw no sign of Freya or any of the hired men. Which was good, surely? The chances were the housekeeper was still interviewing her. Maybe he would remain here and wait to see if he spotted her. Nothing odd or ridiculous about that. An earl sitting in a tree was a perfectly normal sight.

But what if she didn't know Lord Pembroke had arrived? What if she still decided to go to Lady Pembroke and was caught? He muttered a low curse then leaned over to the window, using one hand to slide it up. The window moved. Which really left him with no choice.

It was practically an invite.

SLIPPING UPSTAIRS HAD been easier than anticipated. The baron kept few staff according to the housekeeper, something that irked her to no end. Given Freya wore a uniform borrowed from the earl's household, it was no wonder no one had paid any attention to her while she moved through the hallway of the house. Now all she had to do was find the baron's wife.

The housekeeper said she tended to stay in her rooms with no hint that there was any mistreatment, but Freya could not fathom how it had passed the stern woman by. She suspected the woman turned a blind eye or did not want to acknowledge the lady of the house's treatment. Either way, it angered Freya to no end that none of these people thought to aid an abused woman.

She paused before turning the corner, tucking herself next to a generous plant and making a face when its leaves jabbed their sharp points into her skin.

Men. At least two, she surmised from their conversation. She inched around the plant. One of the men remained at the door to a bedroom. The man speaking with him wore expensive clothes. She sucked in a breath. It had to be the baron. She ducked around the plant when he turned, and footsteps thudded in her direction. She hastened toward the door, her stomach turning when the footsteps halted.

"Wait."

She turned slowly, keeping her gaze cast down. "Yes, sir?"

Several more footsteps then shiny boots entered her line of sight. "Look at me."

She lifted her head slowly. The baron had a thick head of silver hair, his face offering a hint of someone who used to be incredibly handsome. Age hadn't taken a toll on his muscular figure and she could not help glance at his hand and picture what it must be like to be up against such a man.

"Who are you?"

"The new maid, sir." She eyed the carpet between his boots. "Your housekeeper just hired me."

"Oh did she? Bloody impertinent woman." He put a finger to her chin, forcing her gaze up. "Are you discreet?"

"Always, sir."

"I pay well if you're obedient."

"Yes, sir."

He kept his finger under her chin, pressing into her skin until she was forced upon tiptoes. "You are quite attractive in a way."

She opened her mouth to respond but could not fathom anything that would be suitable. *Go to hell* burned in her mind so she dropped her gaze again and bit back any retort.

"Submissive too, I see." She heard the smile in his voice. A shudder threatened to tear through her, so she tightened her muscles. "I like that in a maid."

Bile burned in the back of her throat. She wondered how many maids he'd forced into submission previously. No wonder the house lacked staff. If he could treat his wife so poorly, how would he treat those he saw as beneath him?

Something thudded against the window. He dropped the finger from her chin, and she gulped down a breath, swallowing the bitter taste in her mouth. He frowned, moved over to the window and peered out. "Edge," he bellowed down the corridor. "Have someone check the perimeter."

"Aye, sir." The man scurried past them.

Lord Pembroke glanced Freya over. "What's your name?"

"F-Fiona, sir. Fiona Brown."

"Indeed." He looped both hands around her waist and drew her forcefully into him. His grip crushed, forcing the breath from her.

"Sir!" She gasped and put hands to his chest, ready to shove herself away.

Another thud at the window made him release her.

He cursed. "What the devil is going on?" He thrust a finger at her. "I like you. You'll do a fine job here, I think. Be sure to come to my bedroom after supper. The sheets will need changing."

Words worse than *go to hell* fizzed on her tongue but she bit them back and nodded meekly. "Yes, sir."

She waited until he marched off before allowing herself to flop against the wall. She pressed a hand to her pounding heart. No wonder his wife wished to escape him.

A thud from around the corner made her jolt upright. She peered around the corner and let out a little yelp. Lord Huntingdon glanced her way. She hastened over as he gently closed the window and he gripped her arms.

"Are you well?"

"Yes, yes."

"I was about to enter when he came out of his wife's room." His expression soured. "I rather wish I had now. Then he wouldn't have put a hand on you."

"I'm well," she assured him, "but he is vile. Some of the things he said..."

Lord Huntingdon's jaw tensed. "I do not doubt it."

"Was that you making those noises?"

He nodded. "And now we have access to Lady Pembroke."

"We should hurry. I'm certain it will not be long before one of the baron's men returns."

He took her hand and twisted the key in the lock then they slipped into the room. A woman turned from her position by the rear windows. "What do you—" She frowned. "Who are you?"

Freya stepped forward, a hand held up. "We are here to help."

A red brow lifted. A delicate figure, porcelain complexion and beautifully cut clothing made her look every inch the charming, spoiled society lady. Evidence of her husband's rough hand lingered on her sharp, elegant cheeks, almost hidden by red curls around her face.

Were it not for those marks, Freya would be hard pressed to think there was anything wrong in this woman's life. She even had glittering jewels in her ears.

"A maid? I should think you are more likely to need help than I. I would leave if I were you. This is not a pleasant place to work."

The earl stepped forward and she narrowed her gaze. "I recognize you."

"The Earl of Henleigh, at your service. Your sister sent us. We're here to help you escape your husband."

She glanced at the door. "Not now you are not. My husband is coming. You must hide, quickly."

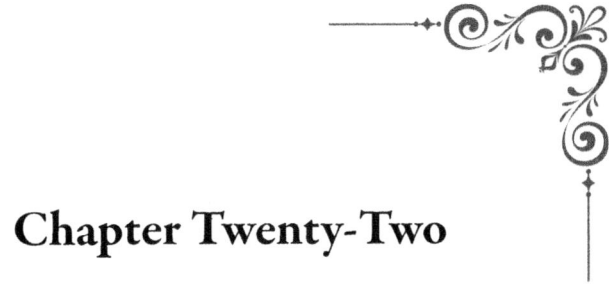

Chapter Twenty-Two

LADY PEMBROKE PUSHED open a hidden door in the wall to the right of the fireplace. "In my dressing room. Quickly," she hissed.

The handle of the bedroom door twisted with a creak. Guy snatched Freya's arm and hauled her into the dressing room then eased the door shut behind them. He caught a glimpse of the baron through the gap of the door just before it shut.

It took all his willpower not to leap out on the man and pound him to a pulp for laying a hand on Freya. He clenched his jaw, glanced about the room and motioned for Freya to hide behind a row of gowns.

He tucked himself in next to her, the silks and feathers cocooning them in a soft, delicate shield of femininity. The baron's voice was muffled but legible. He demanded to know why there was a man's hat and coat outside the house. Guy closed his eyes briefly. If he hadn't been so hasty in wanting to get to Freya, he would have hidden them better. Now, he might have put the baron's wife in danger.

"Were those yours?" Freya whispered.

He nodded grimly.

There was a crash and Lady Pembroke said something Guy could not make out.

"We need to help her."

He shook his head. As much as it pained him, there was nothing that could be done. By law, the baron had every right to do as he wished with his wife, and no one could do anything about it. Footsteps pounded toward the dressing room then there was a thud as the baron flung the door open. Guy moved forward, pressing Freya back against the wall with his body to ensure they couldn't be seen.

Moments passed and his pulse drummed a beat in his ears. Each breath sounded too loud. He tensed every muscle, ready to react. If he had to, he'd get Freya and Louisa to safety and damn the law but it would put all of them in danger, and while he might be able to best the baron in a fight, he was not certain about also taking on his hired thugs. Most of them fought for a living and he didn't like his chances against several of them at once.

He glanced down at Freya, able to make out her wide eyes in the gloom. Her breaths were shaky, her body trembled beneath his. So long as he ensured the women were safe, he'd fight until there wasn't a breath in his body.

Hell, he'd fight for Freya from the grave, he reckoned.

The floorboards creaked nearby. Guy bunched a fist. Silent moments passed and Guy stopped breathing. Finally, footsteps receded, the door to the dressing room shut and more muffled conversation could be heard. Guy released a long breath and Freya sagged against him. He rubbed a hand up and down her back.

"Now we just have to figure out how to get out of here," he murmured.

"The way you came in I suspect. Out of a window."

"I hope you can climb trees," he said grimly.

"Of course." She gave him a flash of a smile. "All reporters are educated in tree climbing."

He gave a quiet groan. "Why do I have a feeling you have climbed many a tree in pursuit of a story?"

She feigned an innocent expression. "I have no idea."

He shook his head and her smile vanished when their gazes locked. Realization of their situation filtered in—his body flat against hers, her back pressed to the wall. Not an inch of air between them.

He felt her small breasts high and tight against his chest, her thighs aligned with his. He drew in a shaky breath and a knot bunched in his throat. It would take nothing for him to lean down and kiss her. A mere trifle of effort. She would let him too. She wanted this as much as he.

Desire raced through him, warming his skin. He clenched his jaw when his cock began to harden. If he remained like this, she'd feel it all.

He moved back swiftly, creating a gap between them that left him cold. She blinked a few times and pushed away from the wall. "Is he gone?"

"What?"

"Is he gone?" she whispered. "The baron?"

Guy paused for a moment, listening. "Yes." Inching open the door, he peered about the room. Lady Pembroke motioned for them to come in.

"He's suspicious," she said. "He will not let me leave this room again for a while."

"I'm sorry," Guy said.

Freya moved to the window and looked out. "Come with us now," she urged. "We can help you hide."

Louisa shook her head. "I cannot. He'll find me and you know there is no protection for women like me."

"What if we could ensure it is not your fault you have gone? That if, for any reason, he found you, you could not be blamed?"

Louisa frowned. "What do you mean?"

"I can arrange for you to be kidnapped. We will take you right in front of your husband. When the ransom is not paid, you shall vanish," he explained. "It will be assumed you were killed."

"He will pay the ransom, I am certain. Besides, I am hardly ever let out of the house at present. How can you even take me?"

"We can ensure the ransom is never paid," he assured her.

"If there is something you are both meant to attend, will he let you leave then?" Freya asked. "Surely he has to keep up some appearances."

"We attend balls sometimes. The occasional dinner party. But we receive few invites this time of year."

"Lord Huntingdon can hold a dinner party," Freya suggested.

He nodded. "That would be easy enough. We can invite you and your husband to my house. That gives us time to take you while you are on the road."

She glanced between them both. "You are certain you can do this?"

"We have done this several times, Louisa. I'm certain," he said firmly.

Louisa pressed a finger to her lips then nodded. "Very well. Let's do this."

"I shall send an invitation out. We'll have to wait at least two weeks. I'll need to get everything ready for your escape and any sooner will look strange to your husband."

"I will be ready," Louisa vowed.

Freya moved to the window and glanced out. "We can leave through here." She thrust a thumb toward the window. "We'll have to be quick, though. One of the men is patrolling the gardens."

Louisa put a hand to Guy's arm. "He will have at least two of his men with him when we travel. It could be dangerous."

He offered a reassuring smile. "We can handle them, do not worry."

Freya met his gaze, a brief flash of worry crossing her expression. He'd never really had anyone care about his welfare before, and he had to admit, he rather liked her concern.

FREYA'S FEET HIT GROUND and she darted across the gardens then tucked herself behind a bush. She motioned for Lord Huntingdon to hurry as one of the men rounded the corner. He sprinted across the lawns and ducked down next to her. They waited until the guard vanished before moving again until they were out onto the street.

She gulped down air as though it had been forever since she had taken a normal breath.

"That was too damned close," he muttered, signaling for a hack. "Let us get out of here with haste."

The carriage pulled up and he opened the door and handed her in then spoke to the driver and climbed in beside her. "We'll take a long route in case anyone is watching our movements."

"Good idea."

She turned from the open window to find him staring at her. She opened her mouth, any words vanishing as his gaze darkened. Her heart pounded, her skin remained heated. They had been so close to being caught and she was fairly certain she had never felt so alive.

He moved forward at the same time she did, and they clashed hard, his lips pressing firmly to hers, his hands roaming her body without apology. She released a small cry at the welcome contact, the flush of desire racing instantly through her, sending a dart of need straight to her core.

She wrapped her hands around his neck, pulling him as close as humanly possible. His tongue delved into her mouth and sought hers, and she gasped as he pressed her back against the seat, cushioning her between the softness of the seat and the solidness of his body. He kissed down her throat, leaving little bites on his journey that made her skin tingle.

"Oh..."

Shoving her coat from her shoulders, he wrapped his hands about her waist. "So damned small," he murmured against her neck.

Freya moved into his touch, arched up and gave him full access to her. The carriage jolted, moving them closer together. He used the opportunity to sweep a hand under her back to scoop her closer and slide a hand down one hip to cup her rear.

His hardness pressed against her. She gasped, twined her hands in his hair and kissed the corner of his mouth, his rough jaw, where his pulse beat in his neck.

"God, Freya," he rasped, tearing his mouth from the crook of her neck to kiss her deeply once more.

He bunched up the fabric of her skirt and ran a hand up her stockings until he found flesh. His fingers dug into her thighs and she moaned.

If he wanted to take her in this carriage, she'd let him. She needed this more than anything in the world. Needed him. One selfish moment of just the two of them, that was all she would ask for. Something to take with her to the grave. One time where she felt like simply Freya—a desirable, beautiful woman with no raggedy coats or ageing parents or responsibilities. No worries about how she would heat the house or pay for Brig's food. Just her and the earl. It wasn't asking much, was it?

Lord Huntingdon released her thigh suddenly. Coldness swept through her. He lifted his head, his hair tousled, his eyes as though he had just awoken from a long sleep. A little red mark marred his jaw where she'd nipped him, and her skin pulsed at points where he'd done the same to her.

"We're here."

She stared at him for a few moments. "Pardon?" Her voice came out breathless.

"We are back at my house." He rose abruptly, tugged down her skirts and straightened his shirt. He rose to open the door and she put a hand to his arm.

"Wait."

"No, Freya."

Her heart sank. He didn't mean he wouldn't wait. He meant no to *them*.

She inhaled, lifted her shoulders and followed him out of the hack, ignoring his offered hand. He shrugged and headed toward the house. Stalking his steps, she spoke to his back.

"You cannot keep doing that, you know."

"Doing what?" he said without turning toward her.

"Kissing me then discarding me."

He spared her a glance. "I'm not discarding you."

"Well, it certainly feels like it." They moved into the house and Brown gave his master an odd look when he had no coat or hat to offer him.

"I lost them," he said gruffly.

Freya handed over her coat, gloves and hat, which gave the earl time to escape upstairs. She went up them, taking two at a time. "It is mightily unfair, you know," she said.

He paused at the door to his bedroom. "I am filthy. I need to bathe. I am certain you need to do the same. Can this not wait?"

Hands to her hips, she shook her head. "It cannot. It will not. I am tremendously tired of you forcing me away." She ticked off her fingers. "How many times have we kissed now? Three times?"

"Four," he corrected.

"And then you..." She gestured to the spot on the wall where he'd given her more pleasure than she'd ever had in her life.

"Do not remind me."

"Am I so very awful?"

"God no." He stepped toward her and took her forearms in his hands. "You are far, far from awful. That is the problem."

"A man like you can take what he wants." She tilted her head. "Why do you not take me?"

"Because I cannot." His voice cracked slightly.

"Why?" she demanded. "At least tell me why you keep kissing me and making me feel all these things?"

"I keep kissing you because I forget."

"Forget what?"

"I cannot be with a woman, damn it. Not even one I want more than I've ever wanted anything in the whole world."

She forgot to breathe. The words echoed in her mind and made her chest full. She searched his gaze. "But why?" she asked softly.

His jaw ticked and he released her arms. She thought for a moment he might turn and run away from her again. His shoulders rose and fell, and he met her gaze once more.

"I am a virgin, Freya. I've never been with a woman and I never will be. Not even you, who I want more than my next breath."

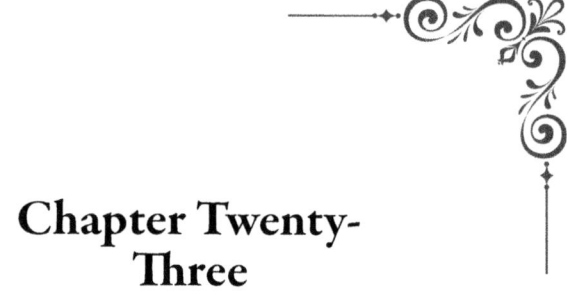

Chapter Twenty-Three

FREYA STARED AT HIM, her mouth ajar. He recalled that expression in Amelia, though there had been a little more terror involved. Most likely because he had been half-naked. He supposed at least his confession was a little better timed now.

When she didn't say anything, he turned, opened the door to his bedroom and shoved it shut without looking behind him. When it didn't slam shut, he twisted to find her in the doorway, a hand to the door to prevent it from shutting.

"You cannot just make such a declaration and run off."

"I do not believe I ran for one moment," he drawled. "That was more like a stroll of a few steps."

An eyebrow arched. "There's no need to be flippant."

Actually, there was. It might be the only way he'd survive this interaction. Now he'd admitted he'd never slept with a woman at the grand old age of five and thirty, she would demand answers. There were few ways to explain precisely why every woman he had attempted to bed had run from him. How did one tell someone he was ridiculously well-endowed? *Oh by the way, I have a giant cock.*

He smirked to himself. There was hardly a delicate way of putting it nor a way that would prevent the recipient of such a confession doing a quick about turn and leaving him aroused and frustrated.

He didn't think he could bear it happening with Freya. He'd be more than frustrated.

"Is it true?" She shut the door and stepped fully into the room.

"Is what true?"

"You know what."

"I would hardly say such a thing if it was not. It's not really something men take pride in."

"I know that," she muttered. "But how is it possible? Someone of your stature, of your looks...you must have had women throwing themselves at you all of your life."

He sighed and rubbed a hand over his jaw. Freya would never let this drop. It went against her inquisitive nature. And while he trusted her not to go writing about his problem in her column, he wasn't certain he was willing to let go of the idea that they might eventually mean something to each other.

Even if it was an impossibility.

Good God. He really cared for this woman. More than he realized it seemed. But once he revealed his, uh, issue, that would put paid to that. No more furtive kisses, no more heated looks from her.

"I have been approached before, yes," he admitted.

"But you just...did not fancy it?"

"I'm not impotent you know?"

"Oh no, I did not mean that." She inched a step closer. "You were...saving yourself perhaps?"

Christ. "Not on purpose, no," he said tightly.

"Then what is the matter? If it is medical, I understand, I promise."

She moved closer and went to put a hand on his arm, but he shirked her touch. The sympathy radiating off her made his stomach turn. Bloody hell, the last thing he wanted was to feel pitied for the fact he hadn't bedded a woman yet. He didn't think he had a huge ego, but could she let him keep a little of his masculinity please?

"It's not bloody well medical," he snapped.

She flinched, shifting back a step. "Then what...?"

"It's my cock."

"Um...your cock?" she repeated, her voice slightly strangled.

He blew out an aggravated breath, slipped a hand around her neck and kissed her hard. She melted into him with ease. If he couldn't explain, he might as well show her. That would put an end to this farce, and he could go back to being the bachelor virgin who ensured he was so busy he never gave women a damned thought.

When she moaned against his mouth, his body ached. He grabbed her hand and pressed it flat against him. She froze and he released her enough so that he could see her expression, his hand still upon her neck. Her eyes were wide.

"Do you understand now?" he said, his voice low.

Her hand shifted a little, sending the most unbearable pleasure-pain shooting through him. What he wouldn't give to keep her hand there, to have her touch him properly. He ground his teeth together and waited for the inevitable.

She'd turn and run at any moment.

Her throat bobbed. "You are...you are...*huge*."

He nodded. "Enough to break you, Freya."

She moved her hand again, explored the shape of him through his breeches. He closed his eyes briefly and tensed his jaw.

"This is why," she breathed. "This is why you kept pushing me away."

He nodded.

"Is this...is this why the engagement ended?"

Unwilling to voice the answer, he nodded again. The last thing he needed was to relive that humiliation.

When she smoothed her hand up and down him once more, he moved her hand away. "Don't."

"I want to."

His heart came to a halt in his chest. He eyed her for several moments, scowling. "Pardon?"

"I want to, Lord Huntingdon." She flattened her palm against him once more.

"Call me Guy," he uttered. "I cannot be bloody lord when you're feeling my cock."

"Guy," she whispered.

Damn. His cock roused further if that was possible. "I'll break you," he repeated.

"Considering women can give birth to huge babies, I very much doubt that."

"I'll hurt you."

"Would you?" She shook her head. "I do not think you are capable of that."

"The first time hurts for all women." He bit back a groan while she explored him further.

"It would not be my first time."

It was hard to decide if he liked that or not.

"I resigned myself to being a spinster years ago and decided I would like to know what it is like at least once before I went to my grave," she confessed. "I know it was hardly the ladylike thing to do but I did not think I was saving myself for anyone."

"I think I hate him."

Freya smiled. "It was nothing spectacular, if that helps."

Great. Now he wanted to show her spectacular. He could bring her plenty of pleasure, he knew that. He had not arrived at this age without learning to use his mouth and hands. But there was still a chance he could hurt her...

"I would very much like to be your first, Guy." She looped her hands around his neck. "That is, if you still want me."

"If I still want you," he muttered. "Christ, woman, I think I wanted you from the moment you started following me."

BREATHS QUICKENING, FREYA tugged closer, allowing herself a moment to feel his body against her. There was no denying it was daunting, but she could not think of anything she wanted more than to be with Guy, as close as two humans could get. The vulnerability in his confession might well have been the complete and utter undoing of her.

If she had not been in love with him before, she was now. It would never lead anywhere, of that she was certain—how could it given she was nobody?—but it did not matter now. She wanted to give herself fully to him, regardless of the consequences.

He put his hands to the small of her back and rocked into her. She moaned while heat flooded through her, pulsing at her core. His gaze connected with hers briefly before he scooped her up and laid her on the bed. He paused when he moved over her, setting his curled fists on either side of her.

"Are you certain?"

She nodded frantically and tugged his cravat loose. He tossed it aside and flung open a few buttons with one hand as he lowered down to kiss her. She rose up to him, curling a hand around his neck and the other curving about his shoulders. Muscles rippled beneath her fingertips and they tingled with the need to feel his warm, solid flesh.

Once he'd thrown off his shirt, he let her explore him, tracing each line and dip of his muscles. He remained hovering over her, his arms shaking with tension, the tendons in his neck tight. She ran her hands down his arms and urged him to put his weight atop her. A sigh escaped her at the feeling of all his raw strength and power as it settled over her body.

He moved a hand down between them and eased her leg up to give him access while his mouth played across her skin. He kissed her collarbone and décolletage and his hand explored under her skirts, seeking out the bare skin above her stockings then moving higher, higher. The first stroke of his fingers had her trembling.

He stroked her many more times until her limbs were a quivering mess then he eased away and left her cold and disappointed. For one awful moment, she feared he had changed his mind, but he shoved up her skirts and settled between her legs.

She released a whimper at the feel of his hot breath on her delicate flesh. He moved his tongue over her firmly, keeping her legs apart with his hands while she twined her fingers into his hair and glanced down at this sensual sight of his dark hair against her pale clothing.

Then he eased his fingers inside her, and she clenched her eyes closed, no longer able to make sense of the world she saw before her. How was it this wonderful, heroic, hard-working man wanted her? She could not fathom it, nor could she bring herself to care.

"Guy," she murmured, and he groaned against her, sending delightful tickles of pleasure surging up her.

He licked her and toyed with her over and over, thrust his fingers in until she was certain she might explode. She almost did. The pleasure built so high that she scarcely recalled how to breathe. Then in one swift moment, it descended upon her. She tensed her whole body then released, letting it sweep through her with a gasp. He gave her a few gentle strokes then rose to align himself with her.

She put a hand to his cheek. "That was..."

He offered a lopsided grin. "Wonderful," he finished for her. He went to kiss her again then paused. "If you have changed your mind..."

She shook her head vigorously. "Never."

A small, relieved smile crossed his face. "I need to see you."

She nodded and rose to allow him access to the buttons down the back of her gown. He made quick work of them, stripped the gown from her body then removed her stays with slightly shaking hands.

She rolled down her stockings and tossed them across the room then put her hands to the fall of his breeches. He let her help him remove them.

She swallowed hard at the sight of him and met his tentative gaze. His throat worked. Feeling him and seeing him in his entirety were two different things. She understood why his fiancée had been fearful, but she knew this man could never, ever hurt her.

Reaching out, she curled a hand around him and he closed his eyes. Soft and hard at the same time, the feel of him beneath her palm had her pulse racing. She released him, laid back and offered out her hands.

"Take me," she whispered.

He nodded gravely, settling between her legs. He twined his fingers with hers, urged her hands above her and locked their fingers. His gaze never left hers.

"Tell me," he said, his voice gravelly. "Tell me if you need me to stop."

"Take me," she begged again.

His eyes were dark, his brow furrowed. He moved forward tentatively, and she widened her legs to him, latching around his hips. He eased forward the tiniest bit then a little more. She gasped at the feel of him and tightened her grip on his hands.

Waiting a moment, his gaze explored hers and she refused to look away, refused to close her eyes to the pleasure. If she could give him anything in return for all his kindness, it was no fear, no doubt.

Finally, he moved again, sinking deeper, slowly deeper. She moaned. He filled her completely and she gulped down several deep breaths.

"That feels..." She struggled for air for a moment, feeling so full, so complete. "That feels amazing."

The furrows in his brow eased and she heard him release a breath. "It does."

He shifted inside her, the length of him sending shooting pleasure mixed with the tiniest tinge of pain through her. Somehow, it combined to create the most erotic sensation inside her. She feared she would come apart in mere moments.

"You are too beautiful," he said between kisses as he rocked inside her. "I fear I cannot control myself."

"Then do not," she urged, squeezing his fingers.

He kissed her hard, moved up and watched her as he surged forward. She rose her hips to meet his thrusts and gasped at the sensations. He shifted against her, more firmly each time, until the pleasure wrapped itself about her and she tilted her head, closed her eyes and let it explode over her in wonderful sparks of bliss.

He dropped his head to the crook of her neck, groaned and eased himself out of her. Releasing her hands, he came to completion against her thigh while he muttered her name.

Freya ran trembling hands over the taut muscles of his shoulders then cupped his face to urge him to look at her. "Thank you."

He shook his head and kissed her gently. "I think I should be the one to thank you."

He collapsed against her, his head upon her chest. She stroked his face, his hair. If she had been in doubt before, she wasn't now. She loved this man, this earl.

Unfortunately for her, it would never go anywhere. Penniless reporters with no noble blood in their veins did not marry earls.

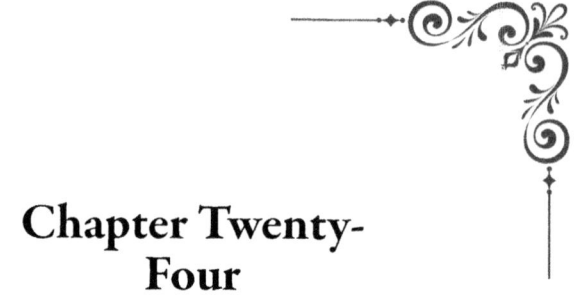

Chapter Twenty-Four

"OH LORD HUNTINGDON!"

Guy winced and drew the perambulator to a halt. He should never have brought Brig to the park. What had he been thinking? Apparently losing one's virginity also meant losing one's mind. Since Freya had left early this morning to assist Miss Walker at the shop and pursue some mysterious lead, work has been damned near impossible. So why not test out the nearly finished perambulator?

Fool.

"Lady Marston." He greeted her with a tip of his hat. "Forgive me but I must—"

She blocked his path with her rather formidable form. Dressed in mourning wear ever since the death of her husband over ten years ago, she struck him as a little like a crow, waiting to swoop down and ravage whatever pickings were left of him.

After a long stroll around the park, there wasn't much remaining. It seemed a gentleman with a perambulator struck a note with every woman from here to Christendom. If a man wanted female attention, this thing was a damned miracle worker.

"I did not realize your brother had sired a child." She moved around the pram and peered in. "Oh. It's—" She drew out her spectacles and pressed them to her face then leaned over the pram.

"A dog, my lady. It's a dog," he said wearily.

"A dog." She straightened and tucked her glasses into the folds of her immense fur-trimmed coat. "Goodness." With a frown, she glanced at him, back at the pram then eased away. "Well, um, good day to you, my lord. Enjoy your, uh, walk."

Sighing, he pressed on. All he had to do now was get to the other side of the park unhindered. If he walked at a pace, surely no one else would stop him?

"Lord Huntingdon!"

He bit back the temptation to utter a string of curse words. His stomach gave a little twist and he turned with a forced smile. A while ago, Amelia's sunny expression would have wrenched his heart, but when he looked upon her pretty features and tightly curled auburn ringlets, he felt...well...nothing. She dragged her husband over, a tall, wiry chap with a shock of almost white hair peeking out from beneath his hat and a thick moustache to match. They went rather well together, he had to admit.

"Mrs. King. Mr. King." He greeted them both. "I'm in rather a—"

"I know you did not have a baby so who is this?" Amelia loosened her hold on her husband, stepped forward and leaned over, the feathers on her hat bobbing in the wind. She dressed with all the elegance and beauty of their courting days but Guy could only think of how Freya would look in such clothing.

Foolish probably. If it were not for the fact the blasted thing was so riddled with holes, he'd prefer her in her ugly brown coat. No fuss, no silly feathers and no distraction from everything that was Freya.

"It's a dog," she said, a sudden laugh escaping her. "Why are you pushing a dog around, Guy?"

"He likes the park," he responded, keeping his expression blank. "He gets bored at home otherwise."

"Are you quite well?" Amelia tilted her head and eyed him for a few moments. "I know our failed engagement took its toll on you and I am sorry for any pain I caused you."

"I'm quite well," he assured her. "Better than ever."

"Good." She offered a quick smile, leaning in farther over the pram and whispering, "I'm sorry that I upset you about the, um, you know..." She glanced briefly at his breeches. "It was not very dignified of me."

"Think nothing of it."

"I think it was for the best, though. You were always so busy, and I do rather like attention, you know."

He allowed himself a brief smile. She wasn't wrong. "I hope you are happy with Mr. King."

"Oh yes." She straightened and offered a hand to her husband. "You are quite devoted to me, are you not, Mr. King?"

Her husband offered a tolerant smile. "I am indeed, my love."

"That's good to hear. Now if you will excuse me, I must continue to walk the dog, or he will get grumpy."

Amelia gave him a bemused look before saying her farewells. Guy resumed his quick pace, the large stone arch at the entrance of the park beckoning to him. Just a few more yards and he would be free. The perambulator worked, Brig seemed to quite enjoy it, and he would never have to experience this again.

That was, unless Freya wanted company. He'd tolerate odd looks and confused conversations if she decided she might want him by her side. He damned well hoped so. He didn't need hundreds of women to compare her to. He knew, deep in his gut, what they had together did not come along often, if ever.

He just had to figure out what to do about it. They were, after all, rather different.

At least in terms of status and history. Not to mention her job. An earl with a gossip columnist? It would certainly set tongues wagging. But tongues had wagged about him before and he'd survived just fine. Freya would be worth every ounce of talk that came with it.

He eyed the entrance and picked up the pace. With any luck, Freya would be home before long. Not that it was really her home, of course, but—

"What are you doing?"

He froze, tightening his grip on the handle, then turned. He let his shoulders sag. "Only you could talk to me in such a way and get away with it."

"OH DO FORGIVE ME, MY lord." Freya pressed a hand to her chest and offered a deep curtsey.

"Stand up," he muttered, his amused expression belying the annoyance in his voice. "How did you know I was here?"

"Brown told me you had come to the park."

"I wanted to test the perambulator and your father kindly let me borrow The Brigadier."

She ran a hand over the wooden side. "It's beautiful."

"It needs a few tweaks. One of the wheels is a little stiff."

She looked up at him and shook her head. Guy spending so long on something just for her was hard to believe. "It's wonderful, thank you."

"Keep looking at me like that and I'll make you a hundred perambulators."

She widened her eyes. "Looking at you like what?"

He gestured vaguely at her. "With those eyes."

"I'm to stop looking at you...with my eyes?"

"You know what I mean," he grumbled.

"I'm not at all sure I do but never mind. Shall we walk a little more? Brig looks as though he would not mind another loop."

"Just be prepared for stupid questions."

Freya chuckled and decided against asking him why he would say such a thing just in case *that* was a stupid question too.

"What have you been up to today?" he asked.

"Well, as you know, I was pursuing a story about this rather dashing earl, but it seems there is no story at all."

"I'm sorry about that." He frowned. "At least sort of. I am not sorry you have decided to no longer write about me, that's for certain."

"It would have made quite the story," she said with a sigh. "Just imagine in it. *Member of the ton kidnaps noble ladies*. It would have made quite the stir."

"I'd rather not imagine if it is all right with you."

"It would have made my career."

He paused and eyed her. "I know. We'll find you another story."

"You do not need to do anything, Guy." She put a hand to his arm. "For once in your life, you need not come to someone's rescue. Besides, I think I have found another story."

"Already?"

"Well, I happened upon it when I was doing a little research into the awful baron."

"Indeed. What is it?"

She pressed her lips together. She still had to speak with a boy at the stables in Banbury, but she was fairly certain with a few words, this story would unravel. "I need to do a little more digging first."

"So you are to keep me in suspense?"

"I do not wish to curse myself."

He peered at her for a few moments, his expression unreadable. "You are quite the woman, Miss Haversham."

"Whatever makes you say that?"

"All that time dedicated to a story and you were willing to drop it in a moment's notice."

"As you said, those women would be put in danger if I revealed the truth." She twined her hands together and glanced at the gravel path beneath her feet. "As would you." She looked up. "I could not do such a thing to you."

He offered a half-smile. "I'm glad."

"Are you also glad I started following you?"

"Let us not go too far," he said with a teasing smile.

Freya swallowed, her heart nearly up in her throat simply because he was too bloody handsome. She had been sorely tempted to remain in bed with him all day, but he had duties to see to and she really did need to pursue this story. There was an inkling of something foul in how the baron had made the majority of his money, most of it having come from selling horses. If she could find out the precise details, not only would she have her story, she could ensure the man never touched his wife again—a little insurance should they struggle to kidnap her before the dinner party.

Her mother's strength was returning too, and she had started to roam the house. The last thing she needed was for her mother to realize her daughter had spent the entire day in an earl's bed. It was almost scandalous enough to be reported in her gossip column—*London Chronicle columnist beds brooding earl.*

No. Thank. You.

Her days as a columnist would hopefully be over soon enough anyway. The new story she had happened upon might even be better than the kidnapping.

"How are plans for the dinner party?" she enquired.

"Mrs. Bellamy is rather excited I think. It has been a while. I doubt she will have any problems putting it together and invitations will go out today." He paused. "We'll have to make a show of it should anything go wrong. We cannot have Lord Pembroke suspecting it is anything other than a real invitation."

Freya nodded. "And your brother? He will be able to take her with ease?"

"I already spoke with him this morning. We're used to doing such things on country roads but there are a few points in London where we could take his wife without being seen."

"Goodness, I do not know how you do this all the time."

"I have been meaning to ask. Um, what will you have me do on the day?"

"Nash and Grace will take care of her once Russell and Rosie have her. Our role is to merely pretend. Should Lord Pembroke still come to the house after the kidnapping, we will act shocked and offer whatever aid we can."

"We?"

"Yes. You'll be at the dinner party obviously."

"Not obviously." She shook her head vigorously. "Why on earth would I be attending an earl's dinner party?"

"Because the earl invited you, of course."

She held up a hand. "No, Guy...everyone will know."

"Know what?"

"About..." She gestured between them, her cheeks warm. "They will know why you want me there."

"Because I find you beautiful and clever and charming and want you in my bed pretty much every minute of the day?"

"Oh, how am I meant to argue with you when you say such nice things?" She sighed.

"That was the secret, was it? I could have ended all arguments between us had I opted for flattery."

She gave him a look. "But it will not work. The baron has seen me if you recall?"

"Blast. I had tried to remove that moment from my memory." They continued toward the other end of the park, emerging through the open gates.

"I shall still be there. I'll just stay out of sight. I can even don that maid's uniform again. There's nothing to say I did not enquire for work at your house after leaving his."

His expression soured. "I would rather you were at your parents' house."

"Doing nothing? I do not think so. Am I part of the club or not?"

"You most certainly are," he conceded.

"Then it is decided. I will be there."

"I shan't enjoy entertaining without you."

Closing her eyes briefly, she drew in a long breath. She wouldn't enjoy it either, watching him dine with elegant people between a crack in the door. It served to remind her of their different worlds and she was not ready to acknowledge their differences. Not yet anyway. It spoiled all the illusions that they might be able to have a future together and she was not quite ready to give them up yet.

Not yet.

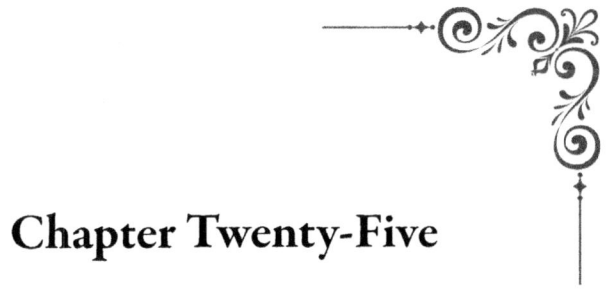

Chapter Twenty-Five

GUY MASKED A GRIN AS his brother made his way to the table in the rear of the dining room of Boodles. Despite Russell's expensive clothing and the fact he only went and married a lady, he still looked unsettled in such settings.

He supposed Russell would understand how Freya felt about such situations better than anyone. He'd gone from penniless orphan to wealthy businessman to the half-brother of an earl. He had likely accrued more money than he and Nash combined, considering he had no expensive estates to maintain, but Guy doubted Russell would ever truly change. At his heart, he was a rough man who had somehow won the heart of a beautiful lady.

Russell tugged out a chair and sat opposite Guy. He glanced around the elegant dining room, designed specifically to appeal to masculine tastes with rich green and mahogany walls, lamps lit at a low glow and slabs of carved wood.

Guy had never thought much about the opulence of these places—they were just part of the job of being an earl—but Freya had him looking at everything with new eyes. How would it all appear to her? The woman who refused to let him have a new coat made for her wrapped in delicate silks and lace? It was hard to picture.

But, damn it, was it wrong to wish to spoil her? Nearly two weeks of always coming together at night surely gave him a right to gift her beautiful things? They both had busy schedules, but regardless of what they did during the day, they always shared a bed. He pressed a finger to his lips. Perhaps gifts made her feel like a mistress. Blast. He was making a royal mess of this.

It was an enjoyable mess, though.

"What's the odd smile for?" Russell asked.

Guy flattened his lips together. "What smile?"

"I knew you were falling for her."

"For whom?"

Russell indicated for a drink by waving two fingers at the nearby waiter. "Miss Haversham of course." He leaned in. "Our newest member. You do recall her, do you not? She resides in your house most of the time and I heard tell that you'd made her a"—he frowned—"perambulator for her dog." His brows lifted. "Is that true?"

"He needs it," Guy muttered. "He likes to go to the park but cannot walk far."

Russell pressed his lips together, eyes crinkling. "I should have known you would fall hard."

"Damn it, Russell, I invited you here to ensure we were ready for tomorrow."

Russell nodded. "Everything is set. Rosie and I have it all in hand. I've identified several small roads in which we could surprise them."

"His men will be heavily armed."

"I know. Nash is going to assist too. Lord Pembroke doesn't have access to a coach, so he'll only have his driver and another man with him. Between the three of us, we'll manage him just fine."

Trying not to grind his jaw, Guy took a sip of his whiskey, letting the warm liquor slide down his throat and quell the unease in his gut. The trouble was, he did not know if the unease was to do with recusing the baron's wife or something else.

More like *someone* else.

"The duchess has purchased tickets to America for her sister. We'll be escorting her down to Southampton once the search has ceased," Guy told his brother.

"We're moving quickly on this, Guy. I have every confidence we can take her, but the baron seems a determined man. We'll have to act with caution every step of the way."

"I know."

"And do not forget Miss Haversham connected you to these women. Eventually someone else might do the same."

Guy waved a hand. "Miss Haversham is exceptionally clever and nosey. I have my doubts anyone else could connect me to these disappearances."

"It might be worth you stepping back after this."

"Out of the question."

Russell leaned back as the waiter brought over his drink and he curled a hand around the glass. "Guy, I know our father was a bastard, but you do not need to pay for what he did. It's not your burden to bear."

"I can hardly deny someone in need of help."

"And you will not, but you have Rosie and Grace and now Miss Haversham. There is no need for you to play anything more than a minor role in this."

Easing out a breath, Guy rubbed a hand across his jaw. Balancing The Kidnap Club with his duties had been tough, allowing little time for anything enjoyable. It wasn't until Freya had come into his life that he even considered walks in the park and long dinners across from a beautiful, stimulating woman.

Not to mention lazy mornings in bed with her.

He wanted more of that, there could be no doubt. But would Freya wish to be a part of his life?

"If you could go back and not be my brother and live life away from the eyes of Society and the gossip, would you?"

Russell peered at him. "Whatever do you mean?"

"Go back to being anonymous, with all the trappings but none of the burden."

"If I did that, I'd have to give up Rosie and I'd rather die," his brother said firmly.

"I thought so."

"This is about Miss Haversham, is it not?" Russell's gaze narrowed. "Are you thinking of asking her to marry you?"

"We did not have this conversation." Guy thrust a finger toward him. "Understand."

He lifted his hands with a chuckle. "Wait until I tell Nash all about this."

"Russell," Guy said tightly.

"You gave him a hard enough time when he fell for Grace. I think he deserves this."

Guy groaned. He wished he hadn't said a thing. Still, at least it confirmed what had been stirring in his gut. Once this kidnap was over, he was going to ask Freya to be his countess.

A HAND TO HER LIPS, Freya smothered a chuckle and paused at the door to listen to the disagreement between Brown and Guy. The dynamic between them always amused her. She hardly knew much about relationships between butlers and their masters, but she imagined not many butlers would be allowed to talk to their employer as Brown did.

"Why would you throw out the newspaper, Brown?" Guy asked.

Freya peered around the doorway to see Brown shrug. "I have no idea, my lord."

"Years of service and you know I like to read the paper when I get home."

"I know, my lord."

"So where is it?"

"Perhaps Mrs. Bellamy threw it away," the butler suggested.

"So now the housekeeper threw it away. Brown, why exactly are you being so obtuse?"

"I have no idea what you mean, my lord."

Guy pinched the bridge of his nose. "Find the paper, will you, please? That's an order."

The butler paused a moment then sighed. Freya slipped into the room and tried to look as though she hadn't been listening in. Brown moved past her and mouthed what looked an awful lot like *sorry*. Freya scowled. Why would the butler be apologizing to her?

A smile lit across Guy's face when he saw her. He waited until Brown shut the door then strode over, cupped the back of her neck and kissed her until she gasped for breath.

"What was that for?" she asked when he eased back and rested his forehead against hers.

"Does a man need an excuse to kiss a woman?"

"Well..." She lifted a finger and frowned. "I suppose not." She gestured toward the door. "What is going on with Brown?"

"I have no idea. The man has been acting strange all day." He motioned to the chairs. "Will you join me for a drink?"

Freya laced her fingers together, aware of her heart fluttering in her chest. She didn't want to say it or even think it, but their situation needed some...clarity. She licked her lips and swallowed. "I was just speaking with my mother."

"She's not unwell, is she?" He moved to the door. "I'll fetch the doctor."

"No, no." She gripped his forearm. "She's quite well. In fact, incredibly well. I think you might have saved her life, Guy."

"I didn't do anything."

"You really did." She eased out a long breath. "But I think it is time for her to return home."

His jaw hardened. "Her or you?"

"Well, if she is not here, I can hardly stay as an unmarried woman without my mother, can I?"

He moved back a few steps from her, his posture stiff. "So you no longer want to be here, is that what you are saying?"

No. She wanted to be with him more than ever. Always. Every day. But how could she continue like this? "My father misses my mother." She winced when his frown deepened.

"I thought you liked staying here. With me."

The vulnerability in his voice dug deep into her chest. "I do."

"So why do you wish to go?"

"We can still see each other."

His expression turned stony. "That sounds rather insipid."

The door eased open and Brown returned with the newspaper. "I found it in the kitchen, my lord. Perhaps one of the maids was reading it." He spared Freya another apologetic look as he handed it over and swiftly departed.

Guy glanced at the headline and scowled. "Why all this fuss over a blasted newspa—" He paused and flicked it open. Freya moved closer to peer over his shoulder. "What is it? Do not tell me the baron's wife has been harmed."

"No." The word came out harsh.

She peered at the paper and her heart nearly dropped to her toes. "Guy—"

He turned on her and waved the newspaper at her. "Is this why you wish to go? Because you were too busy writing about me? What next? Will you be writing of The Kidnap Club?" He made a disgusted noise. "I suppose I should be grateful you only wrote of my visit to the whorehouse and not of the women who needed help."

"That was not me!" she protested.

"It says your name here. Miss H." He jabbed a finger at the top of the article.

"It's another Miss H, clearly. I did not write that, Guy. Why would I?"

"Because your career means everything to you."

"It does, that is true, but writing gossip never once meant anything to me."

"It meant a lot to me," he muttered.

"I know, and I am sorry for the hurt my column caused. Which is why I refused to write it this week." She folded her arms. "I have given up my position there, Guy."

He eyed her for several moments, glanced at the newspaper then looked at her again.

"Do you truly believe I would do that to you?" She straightened her shoulders.

Perhaps she had been right in her desire to leave. She couldn't play mistress any longer—it simply hurt too much to worry about when it might all come crumbling down around her—and they could never marry. Imagine her being a countess! Preposterous. She had rather hoped they might at least remain friends, though, and she certainly did not want to give up being part of The Kidnap Club.

She took a step closer when he didn't answer. "Do you really, truly believe I would do that?"

His jaw ticked. He dropped the paper to the floor. She frowned at it when it landed on the carpet. "What are you—"

Both hands settled about her face and lifted her chin to his. "No," he murmured. "No, I damn well don't." His lips found hers, hot and desperate. "You're not going anywhere, Freya. Not tonight at least. I need you too much."

All resolve vanished at his words. She curved her hands around his neck. "I need you too."

Too much probably.

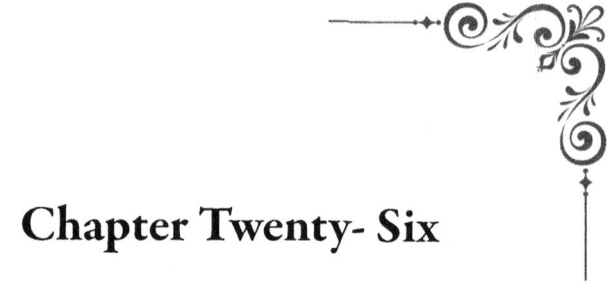

Chapter Twenty- Six

"IS YOUR MOTHER SETTLED at home now?" Guy heard Brown ask Freya.

Guy peered around the doorway, spying his butler in the dining room. Set for the dinner party, candles gleamed and cutlery caught the light, polished to perfection. They had left nothing to chance, even inviting several other guests in case Pembroke should ask around. Guy flicked open his pocket watch, snapped it shut when he noted a mere minute had passed since he opened it last and stuffed it back into his waistcoat pocket.

He ground his teeth together. Not long now and Russell would be snatching Louisa. His gut twinged. He didn't like it for some reason.

"My mother is doing wonderfully, thank you, Mr. Brown."

Maybe that's the reason his gut twinged and had less to do with the kidnapping and more to do with Freya's mother returning home this morning.

Meaning Freya had no legitimate reason to stay. Unless, of course, he gave her a reason to...

"I wondered at you not attending the dinner tonight, Miss Haversham. I should have thought His Lordship would wish for you to attend. I gathered Mrs. Russell rather enjoys your company."

Guy shook his head. He did not know Brown had a liking for gossip. It seemed he did not know his butler at all, even after all these years of service. Guy moved into the room and cleared his throat. Brown met his gaze calmly, apparently entirely unperturbed about being caught with his nose in his master's business.

"Is everything set, Brown?" he demanded.

The butler dipped his head. "Of course, my lord. The footmen shall be ready as soon as your guests arrive."

"Thank you, Brown." He glared at the butler. "That will be all."

Brown glanced briefly at Freya, gave Guy a knowing smile and departed the room. Guy waited a few moments until certain Brown was not snooping around the corner just as he had been.

"Perhaps you should be home with your mother." He yanked out his pocket watch and flicked it open. "I do not like the idea of you being around the baron. What if he should recognize you?"

"Well, that is precisely why I am not attending the dinner party."

"I bloody wish you were. My guest list is a bore."

She put a hand to his, urging him to put away the watch. "I shall stay out of sight."

"I regret keeping up this dinner party pretense. How am I meant to enjoy the night when you are tucked away in some corner somewhere?"

"It was the right thing to do. If the baron had any queries about his sudden invitation, your guest list is comprised of several ambitious men and their wives. I'm certain a man like the baron should be interested in what you have to say. No doubt he expects you to be talking of some kind of speculation."

"I shall have little to say indeed but with any luck the baron shall ruin it all with news of his wife's kidnap and we can send everyone home."

"You can send everyone home," she corrected.

You. Yes. A bitter taste lingered in his mouth. He would be alone tonight for the first time in weeks. He didn't like it one jot. He'd thought to wait until after the kidnapping to ask her but even after the dinner party seemed too far away.

"Freya—"

"If the dinner party goes ahead and all is well, I shall slip out later."

He made a noise.

"What is the matter?"

"I do not like it. You slipping out like some sort of secret..." He waved a hand.

"Lover?" she suggested.

"Well, yes," he said tightly.

"Guy, I am happy to stay to ensure all is well. I should not like to be at home worrying for you all."

"Perhaps I should have gone and aided them."

"You said it yourself, you are far too easily recognizable. Besides Russell knows what he is doing, does he not?"

Guy nodded grimly. His brother had commanded all the kidnappings, successfully too if one did not count accidentally kidnapping his now-wife. Guy always kept himself distant from it all and for good reason. Even masked, an earl like himself was easily identified.

"I still do not like it," he muttered. "We have moved too quickly."

"If we did not, Louisa could be killed." She gave a tight smile. "I think it right that we act now."

"I hope you're right."

She put a hand to his cheek and Guy forgot the tension tangling around him briefly. "All will be well," she assured him.

It would be. Once this bloody thing was over and Louisa was safe, and he could ask Freya to be his. Always. He lowered his mouth to hers and she made a little sound of appreciation. Now was not the time to get lost in her but damn, she tasted too sweet, too tempting.

The tension snaking around him loosened and he slipped an arm about her waist to pull her closer then pressed the kiss deeper. She settled into his arms and he groaned. One kiss wasn't enough. It never would be. He had to make her his, in every sense of the word. She might have more humble beginnings than most countesses, but she had wit, determination and the kindest heart he had ever seen. If that did not equal one impressive countess, he didn't know what would.

When he drew back, her lips were rosy and plump, her lids slightly heavy. "This is going to be the worst evening ever," he murmured. "I have no desire to send you away."

"I have no desire to go away either."

"Then do not," he blurted.

Blast. This was not how one went about proposing to a woman as special as Freya.

"I cannot stay, you know that," she said softly. "We did not discuss what would happen when my mother returned home but—"

"I'm not letting you go," he said tightly.

"Well, I thought perhaps—"

"You could marry me."

She blinked at him a few times, her lips parted. "Marry?"

A crash from the hallway prevented a response. He scowled. "Let me see what that was." He gestured for Freya to remain. "We'll continue this in a moment."

He stepped into the hallway to find Brown crumpled on the floor by the door. He glanced at the three men in the room and met the baron's gaze. "What the devil is this about?"

FREYA PRESSED A HAND to her chest when she spied the baron, surrounded by men, all of whom would look more at home in the whorehouse than Guy's elegant hallway. The three of them stood about as tall as Guy, their clothes refined but worn as though they were uncomfortable in such garments. One black-haired man had a scar across his cheek, a slice of white across a dusky complexion. The redheaded man's face was riddled with evidence of surviving a bout of pox. Behind them, a third, wiry fellow with dark hair revealed gappy teeth when he tugged forward Louisa.

Biting back a gasp, Freya curled her hand around the edge of the doorway. Louisa stumbled forward and her husband gripped her arm, thrusting her forward.

"It seems you want my wife, my lord. Well, here she is."

"What is this about, Pembroke, and why have you assaulted my butler?"

"I knew there was something odd about our invitation here," Pembroke said. "And I knew my lovely wife was up to something. She was being unusually obedient, is that not right, Louisa?" He hauled her close, squeezing her tight against him until she gasped.

Freya swallowed hard. Something had gone wrong but what should she do? She couldn't dash downstairs and demand someone run for help without being spotted.

Guy lifted his hands. "I am not certain what is going on here, Pembroke, but I think you should leave. You and your men."

"I found some clothing outside my house," Pembroke said with a sly smile. "A hat and coat. Expensive garments. The sort of thing an earl might wear."

"What the devil are you talking about?"

"Items that belong to you when you were sneaking in to visit with my wife, no doubt."

"Lawrence, please," Louisa protested, "that simply is not true. I would never betray you."

"Shut up." The baron gripped her hair and yanked it back, forcing her to meet his gaze. "You were hoping to run into his arms, were you not?"

Guy took a step forward. "I will not have you hurting a woman in my house."

The three men behind the baron moved closer. Freya saw Guy glance between them, weighing up his options. Her heart beat a frantic pace. She couldn't stay here and do nothing but how much help would she be against so many men?

"This woman is my wife," the baron said through gritted teeth. "And she will remain that way. You can send all the men you like, Huntingdon, but you shall never have her."

"I have no idea what you are talking about, Pembroke. I have no desire to claim your wife."

"Oh." The baron's expression grew menacing. "So you did not arrange for your brother to hold up my carriage then?"

Freya's heart dropped into her toes. Something must have happened to Russell and the others. She released a shaky breath. They could not wait in the hope that they turn up and help. It was just the two of them.

Guy drew himself up to his full height. "Pembroke, I do not know what you think you are doing, arriving at my house with these men and throwing these accusations about, but I can tell you that they will not stand. Should you wish to discuss your issues with me like gentlemen, I would welcome an audience with you at a more suitable time. As it is, I have a dinner party to prepare for, but I think perhaps you should return home. It does not seem that you are in the right frame of mind to be a guest in my house."

Pembroke laughed. "A gentleman would not try to steal another man's wife."

"I told you, Pembroke, I have no desire to take your wife."

"Did he visit you, my dear?" He tugged on Louisa's hair again. "Met you in your bedroom perhaps while I was out. Did you make wild, passionate love?" Pembroke looked to Guy. "I knew it as soon as I unmasked your brother. You invited me here to get to my wife."

"What the devil are you blathering about, Pembroke?"

The baron made a subtle gesture behind him, one Freya did not think Guy had seen. Her stomach rolled. One of the men handed over a pistol.

"I took care of your brother and I shall take care of you." The baron curled his lip. "And my wife too, seeing as she cannot behave herself." Louisa whimpered when he pulled harder on her hair.

Freya rushed forward when Pembroke drew out the pistol, aiming it at Guy. "No!" She pushed herself between the barrel of the gun and Guy.

"Freya, what are you doing?" Guy asked, grabbing her arm and forcing her back.

She remained unmoving and lifted her chin to view the baron. His gaze narrowed and she saw recognition spark. "The maid..." He looked to Guy. "Good God, you are a clever bastard. Hoped to get someone inside my household to help you with your sordid affair, did you?"

"It was nothing to do with him. I was there to investigate you." Freya lifted her chin. "I'm a journalist."

"I'm not interested in a silly little maid." Pembroke shook his head, released his grip on Louisa and shoved Freya aside. She stumbled a few steps and righted herself. "It is *you* I want." He gestured to Guy. "If you want my wife so badly, you can have her.

Forever." He gestured with the pistol. "First I shall kill you, then Louisa." He sighed. "And looks like I'll have to kill your pretty maid too."

"Like hell," Guy said through gritted teeth.

Freya darted forward as he lifted the pistol. She snatched Louisa's arm and tugged her to one side while Pembroke was distracted. Guy stepped swiftly in front, using his body to shield them both.

Pembroke peered between them all and relaxed his finger on the trigger. "You cannot save her, Henleigh."

"You cannot kill a peer of the realm and get away with it."

The baron scoffed. "I'm only protecting my property and these men will confirm it was a matter of honor."

Freya glanced at Louisa's fearful expression and clasped the woman close. She had no doubt Louisa's husband would kill all of them if he got the chance. The man was utterly insane. Somehow, they would have to make sure he didn't get the chance.

"Go," Guy muttered. "Run."

Freya hesitated. She couldn't leave him, but she had to get Louisa to safety.

Pembroke's smile widened. "Or stay and we can have some fun." He tried to inch around Guy to grab at Freya, but she darted back toward the stairs, taking Louisa with her. Guy put himself in front of them once more.

"You'll have to go through me first," Guy said, his jaw set. "Run!" he ordered.

"I'll catch you," she heard the baron call after them.

Freya didn't wait any longer. Guy would save them. She knew this man and she knew how strong and heroic he was. He would protect them. She took Louisa's arm and dashed upstairs with her, sparing the briefest glance back and uttering up a quick prayer for Guy's safety. She could not lose him.

Chapter Twenty-Seven

GAZE FIXED UPON THE pistol pointed at his gut, Guy flexed his fists. His palms were clammy. He needed to buy as much time as possible for Freya and Louisa. Easier said than done when outnumbered and outgunned. He gritted his teeth. Why had he not been more prepared? Why hadn't he gone with his brother? Damn it, he didn't even know if Russell still lived. He'd been so wrapped up in getting this kidnap done and proposing to Freya, he'd lost his edge.

Well, he'd rectify that now. No matter what, the baron would not lay his hands on either woman.

"I suggest you move, my lord. I do not want to fire upon you, but I will do what I must to protect my property." Pembroke motioned with his gun.

"If you really wished to protect your property, you would not harm her in the first place."

Pembroke bared his teeth. "I am well within my rights to do what I must to discipline her." His gaze narrowed. "Do not tell me you are one of those men who think women should be left unchecked?"

"Unchecked and untouched."

The baron made a disgusted sound. "You might think that my wife would come running back into your arms with your soft words, but I *know* her. I know what she needs." He gestured with the weapon again. "Now step aside."

"Pembroke, you are in my home, aiming a weapon at a peer of the realm. This will not end well for you."

"I'm protecting my property. Property that it seems you have been touching."

Guy shook his head, easing both palms up. "I told you, I have no interest in your wife."

"No man would go to such lengths to get to her otherwise."

"We can do this like gentlemen," Guy suggested. "A duel."

He snorted. "So you can warm my wife's bed when I'm gone. Not likely." He lifted the pistol. "You cannot say I didn't warn you."

Guy tensed his every muscle. All he needed to do was live long enough for Freya to escape. She knew London well enough. They could hide out for a while and the others would help them.

If they were not all harmed, that was.

If anything had happened to them, he'd never forgive himself. Though, he might not live long enough to be able to regret it.

Movement from by the door caught his eye. A brow lifted, he watched Brown peel himself up from the floor with his usual elegance and calmness. "May I take your coats?" he offered.

Guy almost allowed himself a grin when the baron's attention flitted to Brown. It was all he needed. Guy whipped the pistol away and it skittered across the tiled floor.

Pembroke cursed and scrabbled to retrieve it, but Brown kicked it nonchalantly under the gilded cabinet.

When Pembroke straightened, he gestured to his men. "Grab him." He thrust a finger at Brown. "And him." He motioned to Guy. "Keep them restrained until I find my wife!"

Guy blocked Pembroke's escape upstairs while Brown ducked being grabbed by one of the men and slipped around another. The tiny man darted between them like a rabbit escaping a hunt. Guy had to wonder where the man had learned such skills. If they survived this, he had some questions for his butler.

"You're not having her," Guy said, his jaw set.

"Move, damn it," Pembroke spat at him.

The two other men came at Guy from either side. The baron inclined his head and Guy ducked the first punch, then blocked a second, responding with one of his own. His knuckles throbbed when his fist met solid jaw and the man gave a grunt, spilling back.

The redheaded fellow stepped forward and grabbed first one arm, then the other. He hauled Guy's arms behind his back and a fist ploughed toward his gut—revenge for the hit on the jaw it seemed. Pain spasmed through him, air being forced from his lungs. He tried to gulp down a breath and break free, but Pembroke pushed past their fight and took the steps two at a time until he vanished from Guy's sight.

He eyed the two men and spied the red mark appearing on the jaw of the man he struck. Brown avoided the third man by dodging back once more.

Guy twisted in the hold, his shoulder joints screaming in pain. He didn't have time for this. He clenched his teeth, relaxed for just a moment then surged forward, barreling into the man in front of him and taking the man holding him captive with him. They all fell to the floor and the grip on his arms loosened. Guy clawed his way to his feet, striking out at anyone or anything in his way until free.

When he rose to his feet, the third man stepped forward.

A crash echoed about the room. Shards of pottery rained down around the man's shoulders. His eyes rolled upward, and he collapsed to the floor amongst the remains of the priceless vase. Brown stood behind him, his expression placid.

"Excellent job, Brown."

"Go, my lord. Miss Haversham may need you."

Guy nodded, glanced at the prone bodies on the floor and gestured for Brown to leave. "Ensure the rest of the servants are safe."

He turned and raced up the stairs before waiting for Brown to respond. He had to get to Freya before Pembroke did.

LOUISA TREMBLED IN Freya's arms. "He will find us," she hissed. "You have no idea how determined he is."

Tucked into the corner of the farthermost bedroom, they were almost as far from the hallway as they could be. But Louisa wasn't wrong to fear. Guy had been seriously outnumbered. What if he they had hurt him? What if he was—

She shook her head. She couldn't think on that. If she did, she might crumble to the floor and never rise again.

She rubbed Louisa's back and eyed the closed door. They had made a mistake coming in here. There was no escape. But she didn't know if the baron had more men. If she sent Louisa outside, would she be sending her into the arms of the enemy?

"Shhh," she soothed. "Lord Huntingdon will protect us."

"You do not know him." Louisa looked up at Freya. "He will never let me be free. He'll kill me first."

"I will not let that happen," Freya said firmly.

Louisa jolted in her arms and Freya's heart skipped a beat. Her mouth dried. There was no mistaking the baron's voice echoing through the rooms of the house. And he called for Louisa.

"He'll find us," she wept.

Freya peered out of the window. There was no sign of extra men but no indication of Guy either. They could either wait here and hope for the best or run. Or at least, Louisa could run. It would only be a matter of time before the baron found them, and even if Louisa's husband had already fired his pistol, it would be easy enough for him to overpower them both. She hadn't heard a pistol shot, which gave her hope for Guy but not much for either of them.

She took Louisa's arm and urged her toward the door. Pulling it open, she peered down the empty corridor then ushered Louisa down the hallway. "Keep going and you'll find the servants' stairs." Louisa's eyes were wide. "Do not stop. Find a hack and go to your sister, understand?"

"What will you do?"

Freya swallowed. "I'll delay him."

"But—"

"Lord Huntingdon will be but a moment. It will be fine, I promise."

The baron's voice reverberated up the stairs. "Louisa," he called in a sing-songy tone.

"Go."

Louisa nodded, turned on her heel and fled down the hallway. Freya waited until the door ahead had slammed shut behind her before darting back into the bedroom, grabbing a candelabra and standing to one side of the doorway.

She pressed herself against the wall and peered down the hallway. Her attempts to swallow the knot in her throat and ignore how stifled her breaths were failed when the baron's footsteps neared.

The candelabra quivered in her hands. Her grip on it grew slippery so she tightened her fingers. If this man had harmed Guy, he needed to pay for it.

She waited until he neared then leaped out, swinging the candelabra around. The baron lifted an arm at the last moment, catching the worst of the blow on his forearm. He snatched it from her, nearly ripping her fingers from their sockets. She cried out.

He bared his teeth. "You could have broken my arm," he muttered. He flung the weapon aside and it landed with a dull thud on the carpeted hallway.

"I was hoping to break your face," she bit back.

He took several steps toward her, backing her up against the wall. Heat radiated from his body and sweat tinged his brow. Freya fought to swallow.

"Where is my wife?"

She shrugged.

"Where is my wife?" he repeated through a tight jaw.

"Goodness knows."

He snatched her arm and yanked her into the bedroom. His fingers bit into her flesh. She swiped at him with her free hand and fought to pull away, but he grabbed her wrist and hauled her toward the bed. "I will hurt you if you do not tell me where she is."

Freya lifted her chin. "I told you, I do not know where she is."

"Stubborn little mare," he muttered. "Women like you need to be broken in. Clearly the earl has not been doing his job properly."

"Oh I know all about you and your dealings with horses."

He scowled. "What the devil do you mean?"

"I know everything." She smiled. "I know how you made all of your money, stealing and ransoming thoroughbreds. I spoke to someone who felt he hadn't been paid enough to partake in such matters."

He eyed her for a moment then grinned slowly. "Do you indeed?" He lifted a shoulder. "Well, then you definitely need putting down. A shame really as I would have enjoyed breaking you."

Freya looked into his cold blue eyes and a shiver ran through her. He meant to kill her, there was no doubting that threat. She kicked out, meeting air, then pulled against his hold. He shoved her and the back of her head connected with the post of the bed, making her ears ring. She eased herself up, but her head whirled.

Pembroke snatched something from the curtain and grabbed her wrists. Once he started binding her wrists together, she realized he'd taken one of the silken ties used to hold back the curtain. He forced her against the bedframe. The wood pressed painfully into her spine while he lashed her to it.

Freya wriggled against the tight bindings, but they would not give. "You will not find her," she said breathlessly.

"Louisa has a kind heart. She will not wish to see you harmed, I am sure." He tilted his head. "But you can save yourself by telling me where she is."

"Never."

"Very well." He snatched a lit lamp from the nearby table and lifted it high. "I shall have to burn her out."

"No." The word escaped her as he brought the lamp down, smashing it upon the end of the bed. Oil spilled onto the bedding and the flame caught instantly. Heat radiated swiftly toward Freya.

The baron took her chin in his hands. "I will find her, and your death will be painful and pointless." The fire crackled and raged, swiftly spreading across the blanket. "I hear dying by fire is the worst way to go."

Freya tore her face from his hold and tried to bite him, but he moved his hand away. Smoke clouded the room so that when he slipped out of the door, she couldn't even see which way he went. Flames flickered up toward the canopy, catching on the fabric there. She glanced up then turned her attention back to the knots. It wouldn't be long before the bed collapsed, and she did not want to be tied to it when that happened.

Chapter Twenty-Eight

GUY STUMBLED INTO THE upstairs hallway, his gut throbbing from the hit. He shoved open door after door and called her name. Where the devil was Freya? He stilled when he pushed open the door to the next section of the house. He sniffed.

Smoke.

His gut bunched and he cursed under his breath.

An orange glow emerged from the open door of a bedroom. He heard the crackle and hiss of wood aflame. Then he heard her call for him.

"Freya!" he called back and barreled through the doorway.

He stumbled to a halt, lifting his arm to block the immense heat from his face. His gaze met wide, fearful eyes, and he quickly spotted the ties at her wrists, binding her to the bed. The canopy and mattress were entirely on fire. Flames licked along the top wooden structure and the foot of the bed, so, so close to Freya's hands.

"The baron," she called over the roar of the flames. "He's gone."

He hastened over and tugged at her wrists, testing the bonds. Minutes more and the fire would be crawling up her skin. Her fingers were already warm, and her skin shone with sweat. "It doesn't bloody matter where he is."

"I think Louisa is safe."

"As will you be," he muttered. He gave the ropes another tug, spying the frayed sections where she must have been pulling at them with her teeth.

His fingers were clammy, and heat touched the side of his face, sending rivulets of sweat into his eyes. He swiped it away with the back of a sleeve then pried at the stubborn knots. He needed more time, damn it.

Her eyes widened at something behind him. He twisted to view the flames eating away at a tapestry by the bed, moving swiftly toward the door. The air had already grown thick and hot. He released a growl of frustration when the ties would not give way then he stepped back. If he broke the bedframe, the whole thing would come down on top of her. There had to be another way.

Freya forced herself straight, tears spilling down. "Go. Please," she begged.

"Never."

"You will be trapped too."

He shucked off his jacket, retrieved the jug on the vanity and peered into it. Half-full but better than nothing. He doused his jacket then slung it over her shoulders. It would protect her for a few more precious moments with any luck. Then he yanked open the drawers and tossed out the contents. Why the devil was there nothing sharp in here? Why were dinner jackets not designed to hold knives and multiple sharp objects? Why the hell had he not been more prepared for this?

He would not lose her. Not now.

"Goddamn it," he yelled.

"Please, Guy. Go." The flames inched closer, crawling their way down the bedpost. He didn't even have moments.

Cradling her face briefly in his hands, he kissed her and stepped back. She sagged against the bonds. He heard her mutter something about loving him. He longed to say it back, but it was too late now. If he didn't act, it would be over.

He eyed the bedpost and the canopy, the last remnants of the fabric dripping flames to the floor. He retrieved a discarded candelabra and slammed it into the post.

Her head snapped up. "Guy, no!"

He repeated it, the wood buckling with a crack, then slammed it once more. A creak tore its way through the room before everything gave way. Before the flaming frame of the bed could collapse, he gripped Freya to him and twisted, putting his back between her and the wreckage of the bed. The weight of the wood forced him to the floor and the air fled from his lungs. A sharp pain speared through his side.

Freya lay almost underneath him, her legs covered by his chest. He grinned to himself, grimly aware of the scent of burning hair. The ties hung loosely around her wrists.

She scrabbled to sitting, blinked a few times and darted her gaze around. "Oh God."

He didn't know what the situation looked like, but it could not be good. He felt the heat claw its way closer, and when he tried to push up, the pain in his side sent a wicked burst of agony through him. Not that pushing up was even an option. Something kept him pinned—most likely much of the bedframe. He could only see floor, the legs of the vanity table and Freya's shocked expression if he craned his neck.

She stood swiftly and moved to lift whatever trapped him, however the weight remained.

"Freya, you need to go," he said calmly.

"No." Another grunt, another moment of effort, and nothing changed.

"Freya..."

"You did not leave me, I will not leave you!"

Boots entered his vision. He recognized those boots. They were marred with mud and a little blood on the lighter rim of the calf. "Russell, bloody take her. Now." He didn't even know if his brother heard him over the increasing roar of the fire. "If you wait any longer, neither of you will escape."

He managed to twist enough to see his brother's face, pain tearing through his side. He spied the beam and the end of the bed keeping him pinned. And the flames. They licked along the curtains and the doorframe, billowing up over the ceiling. The whole damned room would go before long.

Russell attempted to lift the beam, his face contorted with effort. A rumble shook the room and part of the ceiling cracked, one of the beams splitting and dropping slightly. Russell winced, glanced at Freya then at him.

"Take her. Now," Guy ordered.

"No." Freya raced over to him, gripping his shirt and pulling on him.

"Now!"

Russell hesitated then nodded. He grabbed Freya by the waist and hauled her out of the room. Guy eased out a breath, blocking out the sounds of her cries. Russell wasn't dead and Freya would be safe. He couldn't ask for much more than that.

FREYA FOUGHT RUSSELL every step of the way until he swept her into his arms and gripped her tightly. She flopped against him, dropping her head to his chest when he wouldn't release her. Why would he just abandon his brother? Why would he not let her stay with Guy? Stupid, foolish, heroic men. What was wrong with them?

Russell burst out of the door into the darkened street. She blinked at the lamplight and gulped down a breath of fresh air then gagged on it when it hit her raw lungs. Russell set her down on something soft and she vaguely realized someone had put a cloak out for her. Rosie appeared in her vision.

"Goodness, are you quite well?" She kneeled beside Freya.

Freya jolted upright. "Guy is still in there."

Rosie glanced at her husband and rose. "Is that true?"

His expression turned grim. "He was."

"Should we go and get him out?" Rosie asked.

Russell shook his head. "If we had stayed any longer, we risked the building coming down on all three of us." He set his jaw. "He'll survive." He leaned into his wife and winced slightly.

Freya spotted the blood stain on his leg. Good Lord. How he had even carried her down all those stairs, she did not know.

Freya tried to push to standing. "There's time. We should go to him." Her limbs trembled and gave way and she fell onto her rear.

Rosie sat beside her and looped an arm around her shoulders. "Guy is perfectly capable of escaping himself," she said firmly. "He would not ask Russell to leave him unless he knew that to be true."

She glanced at her and saw the doubt in Rosie's eyes.

"He wanted you safe and you are, that's the main thing." She gestured to Russell. "If there's one thing I learned about these men, is they're incredibly resilient."

"I don't want him resilient, I want him alive." Freya swiped a tear from her cheek. "Louisa....have you seen her?"

Russell nodded, his hands clasped behind him as he peered at the increasing glow in the building. "We arrived as she was fleeing. She's safe."

Freya let her shoulders drop. At least she was safe. It was all Guy wanted after all. Near the top of the building, a window shattered. Russell scowled and motioned for them to move back. "We should get you two to safety."

"You should damn well sit down, Russell," his wife scolded. "That leg won't hold you for much longer."

He urged them to move across to the other side of the road but refused to sit. Flames crawled their way out of the building, catching upon the roof. Tears trickled down Freya's cheeks, though she didn't notice them until they splattered on the front of Guy's jacket. How could he possibly survive such a fire? She should resign herself to the truth now. He would die in there.

"There's still time," she muttered. She tried to stand again but Rosie held her back. Easily done given how her legs felt as though they belonged to a newborn foal.

"Guy would never forgive us if we let you go back in."

Russell nodded. "You are safe. That's what he wanted. I'll be damned if I go against my brother's wishes."

Tiles dropped from the roof near where they were originally standing. Freya finally noted the servants gathered a little way down the street. People from neighboring houses emerged to watch the blaze take hold and a few people Freya assumed were meant to be dinner guests huddled by a carriage. A few had buckets of sand or water but there was little that could be done, given the flames had swallowed half of the upper floor. They were forced to watch helplessly as the roof began to cave in.

Freya twisted and buried her face against Rosie's chest. She should have fought harder to stay. Surely it would be less painful to be swallowed by the flames than to be without Guy?

"Oh." Rosie jolted. "Oh!"

With a frown, Freya lifted her head. She scanned the darkened street. "Is it the baron?"

"No. Look." Rosie pointed toward the garden gate.

She eyed the darkness for several moments. Her heart gave a wild leap. It couldn't be.

"Oh!" She shoved to her feet, her legs scarcely holding her long enough to race forward. She half-stumbled, half-dashed toward the limping figure and flung her arms around him.

Guy gave a grunt but wrapped one arm around her waist. She pressed her face into his neck and sobbed. He held her for a few moments before easing her back. "I do not think this is the safest place to be."

Russell hobbled over and aided his brother across the street. All four of them turned to eye the house while the orange glow seeped into the night. Freya curled herself into Guy's side.

"How did you escape?"

He grimaced. "The floor gave way then I managed to crawl my way out of a window." He pressed a hand to his ribcage. "I'm going to regret it all tomorrow."

"You will not. You are alive."

"And missing a little hair, I suspect."

She touched the singed patch. "Never fear, you are still handsome."

His lips quirked and he glanced past her. "I'm glad to see you're still alive, Russell."

His brother lifted a shoulder. "Takes more than a little bullet to stop me."

"What of Nash?"

"In Grace's capable hands. He took a graze to the shoulder but nothing terrible." Russell swept a hand through his hair. "We were outnumbered. I should have put a stop to the plan as soon as I realized but my damned pistol misfired, and it all went to hell."

"What happened to Louisa?" Guy asked Freya.

"She's safe," she assured him. "She escaped before Pembroke even discovered me. He set the fire to try to burn her out and scare me, but she was long gone. Russell and Rosie found her."

"But the baron..."

She shook her head. "He ran."

Guy grimaced. "He's a dangerous man."

"Not any longer." Freya allowed herself a little smile.

Guy's brow lifted. "Whatever does that mean?"

"I have a story about him that will ensure he remains in hiding forever. Louisa will not have to fear him."

"You secretive little minx. I had no idea your story was going to be something so scandalous."

She gave a slight shrug. "I had to find a story somewhere, considering I could no longer write about this dastardly earl kidnapping poor, defenseless women."

"He sounds interesting this earl. Handsome too."

"Perhaps."

He pressed a finger under her chin. "I didn't mind dying, you know. Not when I knew you were safe. Though, I damn well regretted not telling you I loved you."

Freya beamed up at him. "You can tell me now."

"I love you." He kissed her briefly. "I love you, love you, love you." He followed the words up with three more kisses.

"I love you too, Lord Huntingdon." She curled into his hold and eyed the burning building with a smile. Hardly the most romantic of settings but she couldn't bring herself to care. She had the love of the most wonderful man in the world and that was all that mattered.

Epilogue

AN ENGLISH TRADITION it might be, but Guy hardly expected to be queuing outside his future fiancée's house.

At least, he hoped she would be his future fiancée. Between broken ribs, Nash's leg injury and dealing with the insurance for the townhouse, he'd scarcely seen Freya.

He rubbed a hand across his jaw and eyed the back of the messenger's head. That would change today.

The messenger handed over the letter and nearly stepped into Guy with a muttered apology before moving past him. Guy put a hand to the door before Freya's father could shut it.

"Oh many apologies, my lord." Mr. Haversham dipped his head. "I did not see you there. Do come in." He waggled his brows. "Are you here about the *you know what?*"

"I am."

"Best of luck to you, my lord. She's in the drawing room, replying to one of the letters about her story." Mr. Haversham lifted his gaze to the ceiling. "One drop of scandal in a story and suddenly everyone wants a female reporter to write for them. If you ask me, her previous articles were much more intriguing."

"It seems her story has caused quite a sensation."

"A baron involved in such criminal activities? I am not surprised it has caused a stir. Any chance the man will be arrested? He deserves it for what he did to that poor wife of his. Not to mention burning down your house."

Guy shook his head. "I have a suspicion he has fled to the continent somewhere. Freya's story insures he shall never be able to show his face again and his wife will be glad of that."

"Yes, sounds like he was an awful beast from what Freya said. It is kind of you to aid her."

"I hardly need offer her much aid. Her sister, the Duchess of Newhampton, is able to provide far more protection than I can."

The doorbell rang again, and Mr. Haversham released a long sigh. "I wish these people did not know where we lived."

Guy moved into the drawing room to find Freya bent over the writing desk, her fingers stained and a few inky fingerprints on the side of her face. He cleared his throat and waited for her to lift her head but her brow merely furrowed and she waved a hand. "I'll look at the letter later, Papa."

"*Not* your papa," he said stiffly.

Her head shot up and a wide grin spread across her face. She rose and rushed over, flinging her arms around his neck and kissing him so fiercely he almost forgot why he was here. He had a mission to fulfill and he'd be damned if he was going to forget it.

"Forgive me. It has been such a busy morning since the story of the baron was published."

"It seems you have already made a reputation for yourself."

She nodded, letting her hands sit upon his shoulders. "It might not be quite what I had intended to write but the details of the baron's crimes have everyone quite flummoxed. The fact he had been able to blackmail the highest-ranking members of our society is quite scandalous."

"I'm proud of you, Freya."

She beamed at him and tucked a strand of hair behind her ear. "Thank you."

"I'm glad someone finally recognized your talent."

"I think it was less talent and more stubbornness."

"As I know well," he said dryly. "Which brings me to—"

The door creaked open a little farther and Guy narrowed his gaze at the gap, a string of curses on his tongue when The Brigadier ambled in. He turned a few times on the rug by the fire before settling.

Freya smiled softly. "I know what you are here to say."

"You do?" Of course she did. Nothing got past this woman and he had surely made his intentions obvious by now.

"Rosie told me."

He resisted the urge to slap a palm to his head. Rosie had been that excited about the idea of Freya being his wife that he shouldn't be surprised. Why could Russell not have kept the damned news to himself?

"Well—" He went to move down onto one knee.

"I think if you need to step back from The Kidnap Club then you should do so. Though, you will be missed, I am certain of that."

He froze and straightened with a scowl. "Step back? No, I—"

"I would not think any less of you, though I hope you understand that I will still wish to help wherever I can." She pressed a finger to her lips. "You know I was thinking we could use coded messages in the newspapers. It would be safer for you and keep you out of things a bit more. You would have less to worry about. What do you think?"

He blinked a few times. "That's not—" Guy paused. "It's a good idea actually but I was not intending to step back. I admit I considered it for a while. Being with you, Freya, made me wonder if I should not be taking more time for myself, but so long as I can take you in my arms at the end of the day, it does not really matter how busy I have been or how hard I have worked."

Her smile widened. "I feel the same."

"Which is why—" He bent again.

"Freya, there's a gentleman at the door for you." Mrs. Haversham put her head around the door. "Oh, I'm so sorry, Lord Huntingdon! Mr. Haversham did not tell me you were here."

Guy bit back a sigh. "Good morning, Mrs. Haversham. You look well today."

"I feel it, my lord." She waved a hand. "I shall leave you to it." She winked and ducked out of the room.

Freya's brow wrinkled. "What was that about?"

"Well—"

The door swung fully open and Brown stumbled into the room, his hair mussed and his jacket buttoned up incorrectly. "What the devil are you doing here, Brown?"

He mumbled something under his breath. Guy motioned to Freya. "Do not move. Do not go anywhere," he ordered.

"I had no plans to." She swung a bemused look between the butler and him.

"What is it, Brown?" He took the butler to one side while Freya observed them with a raised brow.

"You forgot this, my lord." He lifted a parcel in both hands that Guy had failed to notice. "I thought you needed it before you asked the"—he glanced at Freya—"question."

Guy grabbed the parcel from Brown's hold. The butler wasn't wrong, but he could have done without it really. "Thank you, Brown," he said tightly. "Now if you do not mind..."

The butler dipped his head and backed toward the door. "Of course, my lord." Guy rolled his eyes at the man's wide grin.

"What was that about?" Freya asked. "And what is that?" She nodded at the parcel in his hands.

"This is actually for you."

"Miss Haversham," someone whose voice he didn't recognize called from the hallway.

"Damn it all to hell." He stomped over and slammed the door shut. "No more interruptions."

Freya peered at him, her eyes wide. "What is—" Her lips rounded when he dropped to one knee. "Oh."

He tossed the parcel aside and it skittered across the wooden floor. "I had hoped to do this in a more romantic manner, but it seems haste will be the flavor of the day." He sucked in a long breath. "Freya..." Someone knocked at the door. He ground his teeth together. "Freya, marry me. Be my wife."

She stared at him for a few moments. Blast, he should have tried harder, been more romantic, given her the gift.

"You want me—" she tapped her chest with the index finger of her free hand—"to be your countess?"

"Most certainly."

"I might not be very good at it."

"You will be the best, I know it, and frankly, I do not care one jot if you are the worst countess in history. I need you to be my wife. I love you."

A smile slowly broke across her face. "I love you too."

"Does that mean yes?"

A rap at the door sounded once more. Freya glanced at the door then back to him and nodded slowly, her eyes glistening. "It does."

Guy remained on his knees for a few moments and let the words absorb.

Freya squeezed his hand. "Guy, I said yes," she prompted.

"Yes." He eased himself up from one knee. "You said yes," he said numbly.

"I think you are meant to be happy about that."

He chuckled, wrapped his arms about her, drew her into his hold and wondered if he would ever be able to let her go. He pressed a kiss to her temple. "I am exceedingly happy. The happiest man in the world."

She nodded toward the abandoned parcel. "What was that?"

"Oh, a new coat for you. You cannot go around being a famous journalist in that awful coat of yours. Brown apparently thought I needed to bribe you to say yes."

"Poor Brown."

"The man will be thrilled you accepted so I would not worry about him."

Another knock at the door resounded through the room.

"Ignore it," he ordered. "I need to kiss my fiancée."

"Of course, my lord. Anything you say."

"An obedient fiancée, who would have thought," he mused.

She pursed her lips. "Do not get used to it."

"I would not dream of it."

"Kiss me then," she demanded.

"Anything you say," he murmured before dropping his lips to hers.

THE END

OTHER TITLES FROM SAMANTHA HOLT

THE KIDNAP CLUB
Capturing The Bride
Stealing the Heiress
ROGUES OF REDMERE
You're the Rogue That I Want
When a Rogue Loves a Woman
What's a Rogue Got to Do With It
Waiting for a Rogue Like you
THE WALLFLOWER BRIDES
Married to the Rake
Married to the Lord
Married to the Earl
www.samanthaholtromance.com

Printed in Great Britain
by Amazon